Y0-ABA-356

If he just did his job right, he'd be home for the holidays.

Jack caught his reflection in the window. His five-o'clock shadow was working overtime. He leaned in closer, inhaling the lemony scent of her hair. He shifted his stance, sliding his grip from the back of her chair to her arm.

Jack hadn't been with a woman in a while, and Abby was wreaking havoc on his senses.

Too much time together in small spaces over long hours could do that to any two people. But Jack was a man of conviction. A man of control. And he wasn't about to let lust get in the way of focus or justice. Not now.

Not ever.

KATHLEEN LONG

CHRISTMAS CONFESSIONS

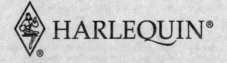 HARLEQUIN®

TORONTO • NEW YORK • LONDON
AMSTERDAM • PARIS • SYDNEY • HAMBURG
STOCKHOLM • ATHENS • TOKYO • MILAN • MADRID
PRAGUE • WARSAW • BUDAPEST • AUCKLAND

If you purchased this book without a cover you should be aware
that this book is stolen property. It was reported as "unsold and
destroyed" to the publisher, and neither the author nor the
publisher has received any payment for this "stripped book."

For Writers At Play with love and thanks for your
friendship, encouragement, cheers and commiserations.
Unconditional love with an endless supply of laughter.
What more could a girl ask for? This one's for you.

Recycling programs
for this product may
not exist in your area.

ISBN-13: 978-0-373-69365-8
ISBN-10:   0-373-69365-6

CHRISTMAS CONFESSIONS

Copyright © 2008 by Kathleen Long

All rights reserved. Except for use in any review, the reproduction or
utilization of this work in whole or in part in any form by any electronic,
mechanical or other means, now known or hereafter invented, including
xerography, photocopying and recording, or in any information storage
or retrieval system, is forbidden without the written permission of the
publisher, Harlequin Enterprises Limited, 225 Duncan Mill Road,
Don Mills, Ontario, Canada M3B 3K9.

This is a work of fiction. Names, characters, places and incidents are
either the product of the author's imagination or are used fictitiously,
and any resemblance to actual persons, living or dead, business
establishments, events or locales is entirely coincidental.

This edition published by arrangement with Harlequin Books S.A.

® and TM are trademarks of the publisher. Trademarks indicated with
® are registered in the United States Patent and Trademark Office, the
Canadian Trade Marks Office and in other countries.

www.eHarlequin.com

Printed in U.S.A.

ABOUT THE AUTHOR

After a career spent spinning words for clients ranging from corporate CEOs to talking fruits and vegetables, Kathleen now finds great joy spinning a world of fictional characters, places and plots. A RIO and Gayle Wilson Award of Excellence winner, and a National Readers' Choice, Booksellers' Best and Holt Medallion nominee, her greatest reward can be found in the letters and e-mails she receives from her readers. Nothing makes her happier than knowing one of her stories has provided a few hours of escape and enjoyment, offering a chance to forget about life for a little while. Please visit her at www.kathleenlong.com or drop her a line at P.O. Box 3864, Cherry Hill, NJ 08034.

Books by Kathleen Long

HARLEQUIN INTRIGUE

*The Body Hunters

Don't miss any of our special offers. Write to us at the following address for information on our newest releases.

Harlequin Reader Service
U.S.: 3010 Walden Ave., P.O. Box 1325, Buffalo, NY 14269
Canadian: P.O. Box 609, Fort Erie, Ont. L2A 5X3

CAST OF CHARACTERS

Abby Conroy—Haunted by her best friend's suicide, she launched the confession Web site *Don't Say a Word* to provide an outlet for others. Yet when a postcard sender confesses murder, she finds herself in a battle for the truth...and her life.

Jack Grant—The Arizona detective vowed years earlier to bring his sister's killer to justice, no matter how long it took. When a new clue surfaces, he'll do anything to get his man, even if that means taking down Abby and her confession site along the way.

Boone Shaw—Exonerated in a string of murders eleven years earlier, he's been nothing but a model citizen ever since. So why has he vanished now? Has Shaw decided to settle an old score once and for all?

Dwayne Franklin—Abby's next-door neighbor has too much time on his hands and too much interest in her every move. Is Franklin a harmless loner? Or someone and something far more sinister?

Robert Walker—Abby's partner and lifelong friend, he believes the investigation is best left to the experts, but does he know something more than he's let on? Does he hold the key to unlocking the truth and saving Abby's life?

Sam Devine—A newspaper reporter obsessed with an old crime, is his interest in the current case that of a man dedicated to uncovering the truth? Or that of a has-been intent on creating a story to salvage his career?

Chapter One

Unknown number.

Detective Jack Grant frowned at his phone's caller ID and swore softly. He put down his case notes and took the call.

"If you're about to read from a script, you can save your breath by hanging up," Jack growled into the receiver, his throat tight and dry from too many hours without sleep or food.

He glanced at the clock over his kitchen table. Eight-fifteen in the morning. He'd been working nonstop since he got home from the precinct the night before.

The caller hesitated before speaking, and for a split second Jack thought he might get lucky and avoid conversation completely. He thought wrong.

"I wondered if you'd seen the latest blog at Don't Say a Word?"

Don't Say a Word? The name rang a bell, but Jack couldn't pry a connection loose from the jumble of facts and evidence his current case had planted in his mind.

"The confession site?" the caller continued.

The caller's voice indicated he was male, older, and either a heavy smoker or someone with a serious bronchial condition.

"Buddy," Jack said, "I think you've got the wrong number."

The caller began to cough—a sputtering, choking sound that made Jack feel as though he was violating the man's privacy by listening.

He thought about asking if the man was all right, but that would indicate concern on his part, and concern was something Jack offered to no one, not if he could avoid it. Concern indicated vulnerability, and vulnerability indicated weakness.

Jack hated weakness.

He held the phone away from his ear until the sound of coughing subsided.

"It's about Melinda," the caller ground out as if struggling for air between choking spasms.

Melinda.

Jack had no doubt there were millions of Melindas in the world, but the combination of the caller's voice and the name Melinda shifted Jack's thoughts from the present to the past—eleven years past, to be exact.

"How have you been, Mr. Simmons?"

"Have you seen it?" the man asked, ignoring Jack's question.

Melinda Simmons had gone missing from a New Mexico university campus not long after Jack's sister, Emma, had vanished from a college fifty miles to the east.

Unlike Emma, Melinda's body had never been found.

Her case had joined a handful of others—unsolved, their connection suspected, but never proved. The man Jack had thought responsible for the rash of college coed abductions and murders had been a self-proclaimed photographer who'd been in possession of photos of Emma, as well as of Melinda and the others upon his arrest.

Boone Shaw had walked free after a trial that had blown up in the prosecution's face. The press had blamed the acquittal on a lack of evidence and an airtight alibi the defense attorney had presented immediately before closing arguments.

Life for Jack had tilted on its axis the day his sister's lifeless body had been found.

Life for the Simmons family hadn't fared much better.

Melinda Simmons's mother had succumbed to her lung cancer not long after the trial.

Her father, Herb, had dropped out of society instead of facing his daughter's tragic disappearance and presumed death alone.

Jack had figured him dead years ago. But here the man was on the other end of the phone, resurrected like the heartache Jack had denied since the day he'd buried Emma, since the day Boone Shaw had walked free.

"Are you near a computer?" Simmons asked.

"Give me a second." Jack settled in front of his PC, clicking the icon to gain Internet access.

He waited for the entry page to open, cursing the cable connection under his breath. He initiated a search for the Don't Say a Word Web site, then clicked onto the site via the list generated by the search engine.

As the site's entry page came into focus, Jack's chest tightened.

Apparently Herb Simmons wasn't the only family member back from the dead. Anyone looking at the modeling shot of Melinda would never guess the young woman had allegedly been strangled and left in the desert eleven years earlier.

"Is he back?" Herb Simmons asked, his voice faltering, his emotion palpable across the phone line.

Jack winced.

Damn Boone Shaw for causing so many families so much pain.

"Could be," Jack answered as he skimmed the site for an indication of just who was responsible for posting the girl's photograph.

Jack remembered now where he'd heard the confession site's name. The Web site and its cofounders had been profiled a few weeks back in *People* magazine.

The site promised an anonymous means for the public to air their most personal secrets, the thought being that confession was good for the soul.

According to the feature story, the public visited the site in droves, their morbid curiosity no doubt driving them to salivate over the suffering of others.

So much for keeping a secret.

Broken promises. Broken marriages. Broken dreams.

As if any of the bull the confessor spouted was true.

Each Saturday the site's blog featured a sampling of handmade postcards received during the previous week.

Today was Thursday. That meant the posted blog had gone up five days ago, and apparently the selected "confession" had been strong enough to carry the site alone.

The faded black-and-white modeling shot of Melanie Simmons filled the majority of the visible page, and included only a one-line caption.

I didn't mean to kill her.

Jack raked a hand through his close-cropped hair and winced. "Sonofa—"

"I thought you'd want to know."

"You thought right."

"Don't let him get away this time." Simmons's tone dropped soft, yet suddenly clear.

"I didn't let him—"

But the line had gone dead in Jack's ear.

"—get away the first time," Jack said for the benefit of no one but himself.

He'd always thought that if he uttered the statement often enough, one day he'd believe the Shaw acquittal to be no fault of his own.

That theory hadn't paid off yet.

Jack might have been a rookie detective at the time, and the powers that be might have kept him as far away from the actual casework as they could, but still, the thought that he might have done something—anything—differently haunted his every moment.

He'd failed to keep his baby sister safe, and he'd failed ever since to find a way to bring her killer to justice.

Jack woke each morning, wondering how he might have saved Emma from the monster that had taken her life. He went to bed each night determined to find a way to make Boone Shaw pay for what Jack knew he did.

He'd never doubted the man's guilt. He never would. And he'd never stop trying to bring the brutal killer to justice, not while there was a breath of life left inside him.

Jack dropped the now silent phone to his lap and pulled his chair close to his desk, studying the blog entry—the reproduced photo postcard, the card's typewritten message, and the weekly editorial.

Apparently the site owner responsible for writing the weekly comments had deemed the postcard a crank.

Jack scrubbed a hand across his tired face and laughed.

What an idiot.

Had the woman even thought to touch base with the local police or the FBI?

No matter. Abby Conroy had just given Jack the first new lead he'd had in years. Maybe he'd have to say thanks…in person.

Jack's gaze shifted from the monitor screen to the calendar tacked haphazardly to the wall. Nine days until Christmas.

The calendar illustration consisted of a holiday wreath draped over a cactus, no doubt someone in the Southwest's idea of holiday cheer.

But the timing of the Don't Say a Word posting gnawed at Jack.

Melinda, Emma and the other coeds had vanished during a ten-day period leading up to Christmas.

Had Boone Shaw decided to resurrect his own special brand of holiday cheer? And if so, why now? Why wait eleven years?

Granted, the man's trial had dragged out over the course of two years, but after Shaw had gone free, he'd never so much as been pulled over for a speeding ticket again.

And Jack would know. He'd kept tabs on the man's every move.

As crazy as the thought of Shaw sending a postcard to a secret confession site seemed, Jack had seen far stranger things during his years on the force.

He'd seen killers tire with getting away with their own crimes. He'd seen men who might never have been caught, commit purposeful acts to gain notoriety.

Who was to say something—or someone—hadn't motivated Shaw to come forward now?

Jack rocked back in his chair, lifting the hand-carved front legs from the floor as the possibilities wound through his brain.

Truth was he wouldn't sleep again until he'd held that postcard in his own hand.

He blew out a slow breath.

Christmas.

On the East Coast.

In the cold.

He supposed there were worse things in life. Hell, he knew there were.

He pulled up the Weather Channel Web site and keyed in the zip code for the Don't Say a Word post office box. Then Jack leaned even closer to the monitor and studied the forecast.

Cold, cold and more *cold*.

Jack hated the cold.

Almost as much as he hated Christmas.

"Ho, ho, ho," he muttered as he dialed his chief's home number.

The senior officer answered on the second ring, and Jack didn't waste a moment on niceties, clicking back to the image of Melinda Simmons's smiling, alive face as he spoke.

"I'm going to need some time off."

ABBY CONROY COVERED the ground between her post office box and the Don't Say a Word office in record time. The morning air was cold and raw, teasing at the possibility of a white Christmas the region hadn't seen in years.

"Good morning, Mrs. Hanover," she called out to an elderly woman walking a pair of toy poodles, each dressed in full holiday outerwear complete with tiny Santa hats and jingle bell collars.

Now there was something worthy of confession.

Abby stifled a laugh and pulled the collar of her wool pea coat tighter around her neck.

The local retail merchants' association had gone all-out this year in an effort to draw tourists into the Trolley Square section of town from the nearby attractions such as Winterthur, Brandywine Art Museum and Montchanin.

Thanks to their hard work, the Christmas holiday proclaimed its approach from every available storefront, lamppost and street sign.

Good thing Abby loved the holidays—or should she say, *had* loved the holidays.

This Christmas marked an anniversary she'd just as soon forget, but knew she never would.

Abby shoved the depressing thought far into the recesses of her mind and glanced at the stack of postcards in her hands.

She'd started the Don't Say a Word online secret confession site just shy of a year earlier, and as the site's anniversary approached, so had the number of "secrets" shared anonymously by the public each week.

Sure, the profile in *People* magazine hadn't hurt. Sadly, it had also drawn the phonies and the cranks out of the woodwork.

Whereas Don't Say a Word had started small and had grown via word of mouth, helping those who truly needed to share something from their past in order to ease their souls, the recent media attention had drawn confessions above and beyond anything Abby had ever imagined, including last week's.

She tightened her grip on the mail as she pictured the card featured in this week's blog. Typically she chose three or four for the blog, but last week she'd chosen only one.

I didn't mean to kill her.

Anger raised the small hairs at the back of her neck. She'd shown the card to a local police detective before she'd published the photograph—an older black-and-white shot of a young woman sporting a ponytail and huge grin.

Even the officer had shared her first reaction. Someone wanted his or her fifteen minutes of fame and had decided to take the sensational route to get there.

Well, perhaps Abby had made a mistake by giving the so-called confession space on the very public blog, but she'd wanted to call attention to the sender's callousness.

The site and service were for people who spoke from

the heart, not for someone who found sending a card like last week's feature amusing.

She'd been a bit harsh in her blog, but so what? There were thousands of people out there with secrets, secrets that needed to be told in order to ease the keeper's heart and mind. Abby wasn't about to tolerate anyone's sick humor at the expense of her site or her readers.

Her business partner, Robert Walker, had wanted her to toss the card in the trash, but she hadn't been able to. Matter of fact, instead of archiving the card in the office files after she'd written her blog, she'd tucked it into her briefcase, where it still sat as a reminder of her commitment to preserve her site's integrity.

Abby crossed a side street then hopped up onto the sidewalk running alongside her office building. The heels of her well-loved boots clicked against the cobblestone walkway as she headed for the entrance.

She glanced again at the stack of cards in her hand, but instead of flipping through them, she tucked them into her coat pocket. The cold had found its way beneath the heavy wool and under her skin. The only thing she cared about right now was finding the biggest, hottest, strongest cup of coffee she could.

"Good morning, Natalie," she called out to the receptionist as she entered the building.

The young woman looked up with a grin, her blunt-cut hair swinging against her slender neck. "Cold enough for you?"

Abby faked a shudder as she headed for the office kitchen.

Theirs was a shared space. One receptionist and administrative assistant for several tenants, allowing each company to share basic expenses with several other start-ups. Perfect for the work she did.

A few moments later, she headed toward her office space, steaming cup of coffee in hand, just as she liked it, heavy on the cream, no sugar.

She reached into her pocket to pull out the mail, but stopped in her tracks when she realized someone had reached the office ahead of her.

A broad-shouldered man stood talking to Robert. Based on the look on Robert's face, the call was anything but social. Robert's typically laughing eyes were serious and intent, focused on the other man's every word.

As she approached, Robert ran a hand over his close-cropped blond hair and frowned. When he caught sight of Abby he nodded in her direction.

The visitor turned to face her and Abby blinked, stunned momentarily by the intensity of the man's gaze. She'd never quite understood the term dark and smoldering until that moment. No matter, she wasn't about to let the man intimidate her, and certainly not because of his looks.

"Abby—" Robert tipped his chin toward the visitor "—this is Jack Grant, a detective from Phoenix, Arizona."

Detective?

She'd heard stories from other Web site owners such as herself about law enforcement trying to gain access to information on certain postcard senders, but Abby had made a promise to her blog visitors. A secret was a secret. Let the police do their own detective work.

"Detective," she said as she lowered the coffee to her desk and reached to shake the man's hand. "Welcome to Delaware."

He said nothing as he gave her hand a quick shake, all business and confident as could be. The contact sent a tremor through her system.

Attraction? Apprehension?

Abby shook off the thought and shrugged out of her coat, then reached again for her coffee.

"Coffee?" she asked the man.

He shook his head, his gaze never leaving hers.

She fought the urge to swallow, not wanting to provide the man with any clue as to how much he'd unnerved her simply by his appearance.

"I wanted to speak to you about your blog," he said, his voice a deep rumble of raw masculinity.

"Detective Grant claims he knows the woman from last week's blog." Robert thinned his lips as he finished the sentence.

Abby could read Robert's mind. He'd told her to toss the card in the trash, and when she'd chosen instead to feature the photograph and the caption, he'd been angry with her.

Robert and she had been friends since elementary school and they rarely argued. She supposed there was a first for everything.

"A friend of yours, Detective Grant?" she asked.

He pursed his lips, studying her, his brown eyes going even darker than they'd been a split second earlier. Then the detective shook his head.

"I never had the pleasure of meeting the young lady."

"No?" Abby took another sip of coffee, trying to guess exactly why the detective had made the trip to Delaware from Arizona. "Old case?"

Grant nodded. "Old case."

Robert dropped into a chair and ran his fingers through his hair. "I told you to throw it out."

"I wanted to make a point," Abby said, her voice climbing.

"I'm glad you didn't throw it out." The detective spoke slowly, without emotion. "Matter of fact, I'd like to see it."

Robert pushed away from his desk. "We keep every card archived. I'll get the most recent box."

Abby shook her head. "I never put it in the file."

Robert turned to face her, a frown creasing his forehead. "Why not?"

She shrugged as she reached for her bag. "I don't know."

Abby pulled the card from an inside pocket and handed it to Detective Grant.

He touched the card as if it were a living, breathing thing as he studied the front, the back, the label, the print of the message.

"Anonymous," he muttered beneath his breath.

"No postmark," Abby added. "I'm still trying to figure that one out."

"I don't suppose the idea of contacting the authorities ever crossed your mind?"

The detective's dark gaze lifted to hers, and for a brief moment Abby saw far more than an officer of the law out to solve a cold case. She saw the heat of emotion, the hint of…what?

The dark gaze shuttered and dropped before she had a chance to study the detective further.

Abby pulled herself taller. "As a matter of fact, I took the card to the local police, who said there's no indication this woman is a victim of a violent crime."

"And they knew this how?"

Abby opened her mouth to speak, then realized the detective was right. A chill slid down her spine.

"You're here because you think differently?"

He nodded as he pulled a folder from his briefcase.

Abby held her breath as Jack Grant carefully extracted a single photograph from the thick file. A black-and-white portrait of a young, dark-haired woman.

The shot might be different, but the subject was the same. The girl from Abby's anonymous postcard.

"Her name was Melinda Simmons." The detective placed the photograph on Abby's desk and slid it toward her.

Her name *was* Melinda Simmons.

The implication of the detective's phrasing sent Abby's insides tumbling end over end.

"Was?" she asked.

"Missing and presumed dead," he answered.

Abby thought about the card and its one-line message. *I didn't mean to kill her.*

"You're going to tell me you honestly believe a murderer sent us that card?" Her heart rapped so loudly against her rib cage she was sure the detective could hear the sound, yet she concentrated on maintaining her composure.

"Someone did. And I want to know who and why."

"Maybe you sent the card, Detective." Abby knew she was out of line, but the detective's holier-than-thou attitude had gotten under her skin. "How do we know you didn't decide to get creative in drawing attention to one of your cold cases?"

Jack Grant smiled, the expression even more unnerving than his scowl. "You can think whatever you want, Ms. Conroy, as long as I have your word you'll notify me when another card arrives."

Abby blinked. "Another card?"

Detective Grant nodded, handing her a business card before he zipped up his leather jacket. "If this is the guy I think it is, he likes Christmas, and he likes attention. And apparently he's picked you as his target for this year's holiday cheer."

Abby took the card, staring down at the contact information, complete with cell number. "How long will you be in town?"

"Long as it takes." Grant moved quickly back toward the lobby.

"What if he doesn't send a second card?" Abby winced at her suddenly tight voice.

"He will." Detective Grant gave a curt wave over his shoulder. "He will."

Chapter Two

Abby slowed as she rounded the corner in front of her townhouse. Dwayne Franklin stood stringing tiny white Christmas lights along the hedges that framed her front window.

"Oh, Dwayne. I told you we could skip that this year. It's too much work."

Her next-door neighbor pivoted at the sound of her voice, moving so sharply he lost his balance and stumbled, catching himself against the window frame.

Abby reached for his arm and he straightened, anchoring his hands on her elbows and squeezing tight. Too tight.

She swallowed down the nervousness her neighbor inspired, knowing she was being ridiculous.

He was as harmless as a fly. A man who'd been down on his luck for as long as she could remember, and a man who'd been a good neighbor to her for as long as she'd lived on the quiet city street.

"How about some coffee?" she asked.

"I'll be right in after I finish," he said with a smile.

Abby stepped back and admired his work. The twinkling strands did wonders for the front of her house. But then, Dwayne kept up her property as if it were his own—cutting her small patch of lawn in the summer, weeding her garden in the spring, and now stringing holiday lights before Christmas.

"I'll leave the door unlocked," Abby called as she headed around the side of the house toward the entrance to her townhouse.

"You have to admit there's nothing like holiday cheer."

Dwayne's words did nothing to warm her, instead reigniting the chill she'd felt ever since Detective Jack Grant's visit.

Holiday cheer.

The detective had seemed sure whoever had sent the Melinda Simmons postcard would strike again.

That holiday cheer, Abby could do without.

The temperature inside her living room seemed overly warm as Abby stepped indoors. She adjusted the thermostat, shrugged off her coat and tossed it over the arm of the overstuffed chair that had once been her grandmother's. She'd love nothing more than to pour herself a cup of coffee and curl up with a good book, but Dwayne would no doubt dawdle and Abby would end up cooking them both dinner.

Oh, well, she thought as she headed toward the kitchen. There was no harm in letting the man spend time at her house.

He was lonely, and he'd proved to be a good neighbor time and time again. Plus, she had nowhere better to be.

Abby worried occasionally that Dwayne wanted something more in terms of a relationship, but he'd never so much as tried to kiss her. She probably had nothing to worry about. Matter of fact, she ought to check her ego.

A framed photograph captured her gaze as she flipped on the kitchen light, and she plucked the picture from the counter.

In it, she and two friends stood in front of a series of

paintings. Abby's first gallery show. At the time, Abby's specialty had been landscapes, her work recreating what she considered the most beautiful canvas of all—nature. But in the years since, Abby had found her time spent creating murals to be more lucrative. Enough so that she could afford to run the confession site on the side.

She refocused on the photo, the faces. Gina and Vicki had been by her side during every moment of her career, just as they'd been by her side during every moment of her life from first grade forward.

Until last year.

Until Christmas Eve when Abby had let a call from Vicki go unanswered and she and Gina had found Vicki's body the next morning.

Suicide by hanging.

Her heart squeezed at the memory, the image burned into her mind's eye as if she stood there now, filled with horror and disbelief. Filled with shame and guilt that she might have been able to stop her friend from doing the unthinkable if she'd only answered the damn phone.

She'd vowed to never again make that same mistake. And then she'd founded Don't Say a Word.

"All done."

Dwayne's voice startled her, and Abby dropped the frame. The glass and pewter hit the granite countertop with a crash, and a wicked crack shattered the glass, sending shards skittering across the counter.

Dwayne was at her side in an instant, taking her hands in his, checking her fingers for any sign of blood.

He held her hands until Abby felt the urge to squirm. "I'm okay." She wiggled her fingers free from his grip, swallowing down the memories of the past. "Just careless…and tired." She waved a hand dismissively. "Let me clean this up and I'll make that coffee."

Dwayne shook his head, staring at her with such intent she felt he could see into her thoughts.

"I'll take care of this." He spoke without emotion as he reached to moisten a paper towel, then set to work capturing each shard of glass.

As Abby measured the coffee grounds by sight and set up mugs and cream for two, her neighbor diligently worked behind her, carefully erasing every last trace of her clumsiness.

Then he stood and watched her work, his eyes staring into the back of her head.

She fought the urge to tell him to go sit in the living room.

He was harmless, lonely, and she'd had a long day.

Nothing more, she told herself. Nothing more.

But she couldn't shake the sense of dread that had enveloped her every sense since Detective Grant had left the office.

He'd called her a target for the postcard sender's holiday cheer.

A target.

Abby couldn't help but wonder who it was that had put Don't Say a Word in his crosshairs.

She'd researched the old case thoroughly after Grant walked out of the office. She'd studied every piece of information she could find, including biographical data on Boone Shaw and information on each of the victims—including Grant's younger sister, Emma.

No wonder the detective wore such a scowl. If Abby understood one thing, it was how the pain of losing a loved one never left you. So much for the adage about how time heals all wounds.

No wonder the detective had made the cross-country trip as soon as he'd seen the blog.

And no wonder he was focused on the question that now haunted Abby's mind.

Had Boone Shaw chosen Don't Say a Word to bring attention to his crimes? Why?

And if somehow the sender wasn't Shaw, who was it?

Abby's stomach caught and twisted as the next question slid through her mind.

When would the next card arrive?

JACK PAID THE pizza delivery kid, then flipped the dead bolt back across the hotel door.

He opened the cardboard box and pulled one slice free from the pie, sinking his teeth into the dough and cheese.

Cold.

The pizza was cold.

Just like Delaware. Just like this room. Just like this case.

He was kidding himself if he thought one anonymous postcard was going to break the old murder case wide open, let alone an anonymous postcard bearing no post-mark.

That particular piece of the mystery had been nagging at Jack all day.

In addition, he'd made some calls on his way back to the hotel. His source in Montana had said Boone Shaw fell off the radar several weeks back.

The man could be anywhere.

Grant muttered a few unkind thoughts aloud, then tossed the pizza box onto the bed.

He'd stopped at the local police department to let them know he was in town and working unofficially. While they'd been more than polite, they'd offered no help, no re-sources.

He couldn't blame them. Surely they had more important things to worry about than a postcard featuring the photo of a young woman missing and presumed dead eleven years earlier.

He'd also met with the officer who had checked out the card on Abby's behalf. Detective Timothy Hayes.

Jack couldn't blame the man for thinking the card a hoax.

The card itself was nondescript—available at any office supply store. The same could be said for the white label, and the message had been printed on what could be one of a thousand different laser printers.

Simply put, the card offered nothing distinctive. Nothing out of the ordinary. Nothing except the image of Melinda Simmons, a young girl the rest of the world had forgotten years ago.

The photograph itself was the only unique aspect of the card, and without further cause, no crime lab was about to waste precious time on an analysis of paper, age and adhesive.

The thought of tracing fingerprints was a joke. What better way to wipe out any prints than by sending a postcard through the United States mail?

Yet, how had the sender managed to avoid the card receiving a postmark? Luck? Not likely.

Had the card been hand-delivered? If so, whoever was responsible might be close. Too close.

Jack took another bite of cold pizza and groaned before he tossed the rest of the slice back into the box.

He slid the copies of his old case notes from his bag, spreading the contents across the hotel room's desk.

Five faces stared back at him from the case photos. Five victims, all struck down within a ten-day period years earlier. There had been no known victims since, so why had Boone broken his silence? Why now?

Jack studied the photos taken of young, vital women—Emma included—during happier times. Each shot had been provided by a grieving relative—a relative who had trusted Jack and the investigative team to bring their daughter's killer to justice.

Jack pulled the mug shots of Boone Shaw free from the file and stared down into the man's dead eyes. Shaw had been a big man, strong, yet fairly nondescript as far as physical features went.

Even eleven years ago, he'd been all but bald, and his round face had offered no unique features or scars. His manner of dress had blended seamlessly into the New Mexico culture.

For all intents and purposes, Shaw had been exactly what he claimed to be—a photographer out to build a business as he helped young wannabe models get their starts.

Jack knew better. He *knew* it, felt it, believed it.

Boone Shaw had been as guilty as they came.

Yet, when push came to shove, the lack of DNA evidence and Shaw's airtight alibi had been enough to let the accused walk.

Jack had waited every year, every month, every day since the trial ended for the chance to go after Shaw again. The Melinda Simmons card might not be much, but Jack planned to work it for everything he could.

Jack flashed back on the image of Abby Conroy.

The woman looked more like a waif than the co-owner of the thriving Internet site. Short and slender, she'd sported a navy knit cap, pulled low on her forehead, the pale blond fringe of her bangs peeking from just below the hat's ribbed edge.

Her long hair had been tucked behind her ears, and her nose, reddened by the cold, had matched the bright circles of determined color that had fired in her cheeks as she defended her actions.

A real spitfire.

Yet her ice blue eyes had remained as chilly as the temperature outside, faltering only when she realized Jack was telling the truth.

She'd been carrying around the photo of a dead girl, and she'd done exactly what the killer had wanted by publishing his message.

Even so, the woman had made it clear her first priority was the integrity of her site and the anonymity of the site's supporters, but she'd no doubt change her tune as soon as another card arrived.

And it would arrive.

Jack hadn't been so sure about anything since the day he'd first looked into Boone Shaw's eyes and known the man had killed Emma.

Abby Conroy might think her precious blog site innocent in the sins of the past, but as long as she encouraged confessions, she sure as hell wasn't innocent in the sins of the present.

And Jack had no qualms about blowing Abby Conroy and Don't Say a Word sky-high.

He'd vowed long ago to do whatever it took to bring Emma's killer to justice.

Now all Jack had to do was sit back…and wait.

ABBY RETURNED TO the broken photo frame after Dwayne left.

For once, her neighbor hadn't lingered. Matter of fact, Abby was used to the man being quiet, but tonight he'd been more distant than ever. If Abby hadn't known better, she'd swear there'd been something he wanted to tell her, a secret he wanted to share.

Abby knew Dwayne regularly read the blog. He'd told her so on various occasions over the past year—while they shared a glass of iced tea after he'd worked in her yard, or on the occasional evening she offered him a quick sandwich when he'd bring over her mail.

He'd never told her much about his life, his work, his past. Perhaps that was better.

The man was a loner in the true sense of the word, and yet he'd befriended Abby. He looked out for her, kept an eye on her property, trusted her.

He even went so far as to take Abby's personal mail from the small box by her front door if she worked too late. He had a fear of the mail sitting out all day.

Perhaps he'd once been the victim of identity theft— who knew—but on the occasions Dwayne did take in her mail, Abby would thank him for his kindness and write off the odd practice as a quirk of a lonely mind.

The fact Abby hadn't put a stop to the practice drove Robert and Gina insane, but Abby knew Dwayne was only trying to be neighborly.

Both Robert and Gina felt Dwayne's overfamiliarity was just that. Overfamiliar. Robert had gone so far as to say Dwayne's behavior bordered on stalking, but Abby didn't agree.

Dwayne was lonely and more than a little paranoid. End of story. And as far as Abby knew, none of the other neighbors gave Dwayne the time of day.

Well, she, for one, wasn't about to ignore him.

Abby dropped her gaze to the scarred picture of herself with Gina and Vicki. Just look where ignoring a friend had gotten her once before.

Vicki's death was the reason Abby spent so much time with each postcard she received. She tried to put herself in the sender's position, tried to imagine the anguish, the guilt, the relief each felt at finally coming clean.

She was no therapist, nor did she profess to be one, but she could offer space. Space to come clean. Space to confess. Space to shed the burden of a secret's weight carried for too long.

Abby understood the pain of holding a secret inside, she understood how the truth could slowly eat away at you, uncoiling like a snake.

She'd never told a soul—not even Robert or Gina—about the call she'd ignored from Vicki.

Perhaps someday she'd send herself a postcard.

She laughed at the irony, glad she could laugh at something today.

A mental image of Detective Jack Grant flashed through her mind and her belly tightened. The man's intensity was breathtaking, albeit foreboding. If he hadn't scowled so intently the entire time he'd been at the office, she might be tempted to call him handsome. But she wasn't about to make that leap, not anytime soon.

She thought again about the case information she'd uncovered on the New Mexico murders.

Seemed Detective Grant had left out a bit of information himself. So much for full disclosure.

No matter. Abby recognized his type.

He'd tell her what she needed to know, when he thought she needed to know it. He probably believed he was protecting her by sparing her the gory details—like the killer's signature.

She shuddered at the thought.

Abby had been too harsh with the detective, too defensive about her work and the site, and she knew it.

The detective had called briefly later in the day, asking to go through the archives in order to check each postcard for any sign the sender had reached out before.

Abby thought the exercise would be nothing but wasted time, but if that's what Jack Grant wanted to do, that's what she'd help him do.

And then it hit her.

Postcards.

She'd never so much as flipped through the contents of the post office box that morning. She'd been so taken aback by the detective's visit and the harsh reality of his disclosure she'd forgotten about today's mail.

Abby retraced her steps to the living room and dipped her hand inside the large pocket of her coat. Today's stack of cards hadn't been quite as cumbersome as those in recent weeks. Perhaps the onslaught of submissions that had followed the *People* magazine article was finally tapering off.

Maybe now business would return to usual.

She checked the thought immediately. Business as usual did not include an apparent murder confession.

Abby sank into her favorite chair and flipped through the cards one by one, reading each message before she studied the accompanying graphic.

I never told my father I loved him.

Abby's heart ached as she studied the apparently scanned image of a scribbled crayon drawing of a house and tree on the reverse side of the card.

I cheated on my bar exam.

The submission featured a store-bought, glossy image of a lush tropical resort.

Apparently this particular confessor didn't suffer remorse. Abby laughed and moved on.

She shouldn't have ignored me.

Simple black type on a white label.

No postmark.

Abby choked on her laughter.

She dropped the card into her lap and reached for her gloves. She pulled them from her coat pocket and slipped them over her fingers before she reached for the card again, this time turning the simple card over.

Surely she was overreacting.

This card couldn't be the same, couldn't be another confession, another photograph of some poor girl who'd thought she had a shot at a modeling career and ended up dead.

Abby held her breath, gripping only the edges of the card as she turned it over.

A beautiful young woman looked back from the black-and-white shot. She smiled, and yet her eyes hinted at something other than joy. In them, Abby saw nervousness…and fear. Had she known she was in danger at the moment this shot was taken?

The coffee Abby had shared with Dwayne churned in her stomach as she turned back to the message, reading it again.

She shouldn't have ignored me.

Dread gripped her by the throat and squeezed even as the bright white lights twinkled through her sheer curtains from the bushes outside—an ironic juxtaposition of holiday present and past.

Abby carefully placed the card on an end table and reached into her coat pocket again, this time in search of Detective Grant's business card.

Her own words echoed in her brain.

What if he doesn't send a second card?

She'd been so sure of herself, even after the detective's explanation of the case and the killer's cruelty.

Detective Grant had been equally sure, and he'd been correct in his prediction.

He will. He will.

Little did the detective know the second card had been in her coat pocket even as he'd spoken.

Abby dropped her focus to Jack Grant's business card and studied his cell phone number.

The man had traveled all the way from Arizona to Delaware to chase a single lead. She had to admire him for that.

Then Abby took a deep breath, reached for her phone and dialed.

Chapter Three

Jack pulled his rental car to a stop in front of the quaint townhouse. Small white lights twinkled from the short hedge lining the home's oversized windows.

Figured Abby Conroy would have holiday lights.

Based on the tone of her voice when she called, Jack's earlier visit had served to snap her out of any holiday cheer she'd been experiencing.

Jack unfolded himself from the car and headed toward the door. *Around the side,* she'd said.

Dark sidewalk. Isolated entrance.

The woman was nothing if not a picture of what *not to do* when devising personal security.

She'd provided him with her home address, but Jack had already been able to ascertain that information without so much as pulling a single departmental string.

He'd tracked her by working backward from her post-card confession site through the registration database and public contact information he'd pulled online.

If Boone Shaw—or anyone, for that matter—decided to target Abby Conroy, nothing about the woman's life would make finding her a challenge.

Now that Jack had had time to stew on the information

he'd received, he was certain Boone Shaw had gone under-
ground for a reason.

Shaw had never vanished so thoroughly before, and even
though he'd never been picked up on any sort of charge
during the eleven years since the trial, he'd left a trail.

Until now.

Business dealings. A new photography studio. Credit
card and mortgage debt.

The man had led a normal life, a full life, a life he didn't
deserve.

A calm sureness slid through Jack's system as he
headed toward Abby Conroy's door.

There was always a chance Shaw wasn't the person
physically sending the cards, but Jack had no doubt he was
responsible. Somehow.

The man had killed Emma, just as he'd killed Melinda
Simmons and the others.

Jack had seen it in Shaw's eyes the day they'd pulled the
man into custody along with the piles of so-called modeling
shots he'd accumulated during his time as a photographer.

The man had been guilty—a sexual predator with a
camera. And his victims had been only too willing to pose,
believing his promises of bright futures, bright lights, big
dreams come true.

"Can I help you?" A thirtysomething man wearing only
a pair of jeans, sneakers and gray sweatshirt stepped into
Jack's path.

Jack's hand reached automatically for his weapon before he remembered he'd left his service revolver back in
Arizona, part of the agreement he'd struck with his chief.

The weight of his backup weapon in his ankle holster
provided comfort, but reaching for the gun didn't fall under
the subtle category, nor was the move necessary.

The ghost of Boone Shaw had Jack jumping like a rookie.

Besides, the man before him was more than likely nothing but a neighbor, someone suspicious of a man approaching Abby Conroy's door.

Jack couldn't fault him for that, but he could ask questions.

Jack measured the man, from his feet to his face. "A bit cold to be outside without a coat, isn't it?"

"I spend a lot of time over here." The man's dark eyes shifted, their focus bouncing from side to side, never making direct eye contact. "With Abby," he added, as if use of her name would prove something to Jack, somehow put him in his place.

Jack extended his hand. "Detective Jack Grant. I'm here on official business."

The other man blinked, his expression morphing from aggressive to vacant. "Dwayne Franklin. Abby and I have a…relationship."

Jack doubted the validity of the man's statement based on his inability to make eye contact.

If anything, the man was a neighbor who thought he had a relationship with Abby Conroy—yet another security issue Jack planned to talk to the woman about.

Jack flashed his shield, and the man uttered a quick good-night as he headed toward the house next door.

Abby pulled the door open, having apparently heard voices.

"Detective Grant?"

"You might as well start calling me Jack." He jerked a thumb toward the neighbor's house. "Does your neighbor make a practice of lurking outside your house?"

A crease formed between Abby's brows and Jack noted her coloring seemed paler than it had been that morning. "Dwayne?"

Jack nodded.

"He hung the lights for me earlier. He was probably checking his work."

Jack gave another sharp nod, saying nothing. Let the woman believe what she wanted to believe. As far as Jack was concerned, her neighbor's actions were a bit too over-protective.

Jack had always been a master at assessing people and their situations, and this situation was no different.

Abby Conroy apparently trusted everyone, her postcard confessors and loitering neighbor included.

Jack trusted no one.

Any work they did together ought to prove interesting, if nothing else.

He chuckled under his breath, quickly catching himself and smoothing his features. He couldn't remember the last time he'd found anything humorous. But if he was forced to work alongside Ms. Conroy in order to flesh out this lead, he might as well enjoy himself.

"Something funny, Detective Grant?"

Confusion flashed in the woman's pale eyes, yet it was a second emotion lurking there that sobered Jack, an emotion visibly battling for position.

Fear.

Maybe Abby Conroy wasn't as naive as Jack had thought.

He shook his head. "I meant no disrespect, but you and I need to talk about protecting yourself."

He patted the door frame as he pushed the door shut behind them. The flimsy door boasted nothing more than a keyed lock.

He tapped the knob. "There's this new gadget called a dead bolt. You might want to check it out."

But his warning fell on apparently deaf ears. Abby showed no sign of having heard a word he'd said.

She hadn't explained the reason for her call, and Jack

hadn't pressed her. He'd hoped she wanted to talk to him about a change of heart regarding the archived postcards.

But as Abby pointed to a stack of postcards sitting on an end table, then reached for one in particular, Jack's stomach caught.

"He's sent another, hasn't he?"

She handled the card by the edges, handing it to Jack even as she spoke, not answering his question, but rather reciting the card's message from memory.

"She shouldn't have ignored me." Abby's voice dropped low, shaken.

Jack forced himself to look away from her face, to shove aside the ridiculous urge to reach for her, to promise her he wouldn't let the man responsible for sending the postcards touch her.

He forced himself instead to reach for the card, to study the message.

The sender had once again used a nondescript white mailing label, printed in what appeared to be laser printer ink. The label had been adhered to the back of a plain white postcard.

Nondescript. Untraceable.

Again.

But there was nothing nondescript about the photograph glued to the opposite side.

Jack turned the card over in his hand and swore beneath his breath at the sight of the face captured in the black-and-white print.

His features fell slack, slipping like the strength in his body.

Abby placed one slender hand on his arm. "Detective? Are you all right?"

Her words reached him through a fog of semiawareness. The face on the photograph fully captured his focus, his senses, and yet he'd never seen this particular photograph before.

Never before.

Jack set down the card long enough to reach for his briefcase, extracting a small evidence bag. He slid the postcard inside, carefully touching only the edges even though he knew the card had been handled countless times during its journey through the mail.

"Detective?" Abby released his arm, but her tone grew stronger, more urgent. "Is she one of the five from New Mexico?"

Impressive. Abby Conroy had done her homework during the hours since he'd stepped into her life and world, something that didn't surprise Jack in the least.

He steeled himself then nodded, tucking the card away before he looked up. "Her name was Emma. She was nine-teen when he killed her."

"Emma?"

Jack shoved down the tide of grief threatening to drown his senses.

"Emma Grant?" Abby asked softly.

Jack gave another nod, not trusting his voice at the moment and not wanting Abby to sense how much the card had rocked him.

The bastard had sent a picture of Emma. A picture Jack had never seen either in Emma's personal belongings or the photos taken from Boone Shaw during the original investigation.

"I'm so sorry, Detective."

"Are you ready to work with me now?" Jack purposely redirected the conversation, wanting Abby's cooperation, not her sympathy.

Abby's throat worked. "I'm sorry for how I acted earlier. I was being defensive and I was wrong."

Jack pointed to one of the living-room chairs, gesturing for Abby to sit. "Tell me what you found out since this morning, then I'll fill in the gaps."

As Abby recounted the news articles she'd uncovered online, Jack leaned his hip against a second chair, and wondered whose face Shaw would feature in his next message. And when?

No matter. Jack was here now. He had eleven more years of experience than he'd had the last time he'd gone up against Boone Shaw, and this time he was ready.

Jack planned to do exactly what Herb Simmons had asked him to do—whatever it took to make sure Shaw didn't get away again.

This time, Boone Shaw was going to pay for the lives he'd ended, the families he'd ripped apart and the heartache he'd inflicted.

This time, Boone Shaw was going away.

For good.

HE WONDERED HOW many people remembered the girl in the photograph—her blond hair bouncing around her shoulders in natural waves, her dark eyes bright and hopeful.

He remembered those eyes in death, still searching as if pleading for her life.

Her parents had died not long after she'd been found dead and battered, her body dumped in Valley Forge National Park. A freak accident in a snowstorm had taken their lives, if he remembered correctly.

His mind and sense of clarity might not be what they'd once been, but his sense of what drew people's attention hadn't faltered.

If he played this right, the Don't Say a Word site might prove to be the opportunity he'd been seeking for years.

One more anonymous card confessing a murder, one more innocent face, one more blog and the story would take on a life of its own.

And there was nothing he loved more than a story—a good story.

A new postcard would launch this particular story into the national focus, and he'd be right there to reap the benefits.

What would the media call the sender? The Christmas Killer? The Christmas Confessor?

He laughed, enjoying the moment.

The Christmas Confessor.

He liked it. He liked it a lot.

He carefully adhered the print to the postcard then affixed the one-line message to the back.

No one likes a show off.

What would Abby Conroy say about this card? Would she call him an opportunist?

Perhaps.

But then, she wouldn't be far from the truth, would she?

He thought about logging on to the Internet and visiting the confession site again to stare at the first card, to study the expression on Melinda Simmons's young features, but he forced himself to focus.

Forced himself to finish the task at hand.

He carefully tucked the postcard into his briefcase, careful not to leave any prints. Then he reached for his coat. After all, the night air outside had gone cold and raw and he had miles to go.

Miles to go.

Things to do.

And *confessions* to deliver.

Chapter Four

Abby started a second pot of coffee while Jack Grant worked in the office's shared conference room. She'd checked the schedule when she and Jack arrived late last night, and knew no one had the room booked for today. It was Saturday, after all.

"I need to raise a pertinent question," she said as she headed back into the room where stacks of postcards covered every available space.

Jack grunted, his version of a reply, Abby had quickly learned during the hours they'd been working side-by-side, studying postcard after postcard.

"It's Saturday. I need to post a new blog."

The detective's hand stilled on the card he'd been reading and he lifted his gaze to hers. "Any thoughts?"

Did she know what she wanted to say this week? Which secret confessions she wanted to feature?

She'd had three cards picked out and her thoughts ready to go, but that had been yesterday. Yesterday, before her sense of reality had been turned on its ear.

Today, she could think of only one message. One card. *She shouldn't have ignored me.*

"I want to flush him out." She braced herself, expecting a harsh response from Jack.

Instead, the detective narrowed his eyes thoughtfully, reached for the outstretched coffee cup and took a long drink.

The man took his time before he answered, and Abby could almost hear the wheels turning in his brain. The depth of his concentration turned his caramel eyes chocolate and his sharp features smooth.

Abby swallowed down the sudden tightness in her throat at the precise moment the detective spoke.

"Do it."

Abby blinked, surprised by his lack of objection. "Really?"

He shrugged with his eyes. "That's the answer you wanted, correct?" Jack gestured to the piles of cards, the thousands they'd spent the night sorting.

Abby could follow his thoughts without him saying a word. They hadn't found another card like the first two, and out of thousands and thousands of postcards, they'd found only a handful of cards without a postmark.

What were the odds the two cards—the photos of Melinda Simmons and Emma Grant—both happened to slide through the United States Post Office machines unscathed? Fairly high, she'd imagine.

Somehow, whoever had sent those cards had gotten around the system, but how?

"He either hand-delivered the cards or slipped them into your post office box," Jack said matter-of-factly. "He's closer than you think, Ms. Conroy. The sooner we find him, the better."

Abby's belly tightened. "How close?"

The detective dropped his focus back to the pile of postcards sitting in front of him. "That's what I intend to find out."

A SHORT WHILE LATER, Jack shifted his focus from the remaining stacks of cards to Abby Conroy herself.

He watched her as she sorted through a stack, pulling at her lower lip with her top teeth as she concentrated. She tucked a wayward strand of long, sleek hair behind her ear then abruptly looked up at Jack, as if she'd sensed him watching.

Her eyebrows drew together. "Something I can do for you?"

Even as exhausted as he knew the woman must be, determination and stubbornness blazed in her expression. She was a spitfire, of that there was no doubt.

Jack shook his head, realizing he must be more tired than he realized. He'd allowed the woman to catch him openly staring at her.

Busted.

Then he asked the question he'd been pondering since he'd first set foot inside the Don't Say a Word office.

"I can't help but wonder why someone like you felt compelled to solicit all of—" he gestured to the thousands of cards on the table "—this. Don't you have demons of your own to contend with?"

Abby's throat worked as if he'd hit a nerve. "Maybe that's why I wanted to give others a vehicle, a safe and anonymous way to cleanse their conscience."

"Because you don't have a way?"

"Maybe I'm just a sympathetic person, Detective."

Detective.

He *had* hit a nerve.

Abby dropped her focus back to the stack of cards, effectively telling him to buzz off without saying so. What she couldn't realize was that her nonverbal response had set off the investigative portion of Jack's brain.

The woman had tapped into his curiosity as soon as they'd met, with her all-American looks and her stubborn demeanor, but now that Jack had stolen a glimpse through the crack in her protective wall, he wanted more. He wanted the full story.

"You're right, though," he said, never taking his focus from her, wanting to read her response.

"Right about the site?"

"Right about the cards."

That got her attention and she lifted her curious gaze, her eyes the color of a clear, winter sky.

"I think Melinda's card was the first. There's nothing here to suggest this guy's reached out to you before last week."

"But you think he'll reach out again?" She spoke slowly, using his terminology.

Jack nodded.

"I don't understand why." Her voice tightened. "Why Don't Say a Word? And what does he hope to gain?"

"That, Ms. Conroy, is the sixty-million-dollar question."

She disappeared after that, claiming the need to clear her head. Jack couldn't blame her.

They'd been working all night and the truth was, the cold, cruel world outside had marched right into her life the moment Jack had arrived on the scene and burst her crank-postcard-theory bubble.

He'd have been surprised if she didn't need space at some point.

As for Jack, he'd finished sorting postcards and didn't care if he never saw another so-called confession again in his life.

What he needed to do now was to get back to his hotel. He had calls to make and a former suspect to track down.

When footfalls sounded behind him, Jack never guessed anyone but Abby would be stepping into the conference room.

He rocked back in the chair without turning around. "I'm not finding anything."

But the voice that answered wasn't Abby's.

"What was it you were looking for?" Humor tangled with curiosity in Robert Walker's voice.

Jack straightened, pushing himself out of the chair to greet Abby's partner. "Surprised to see you here on a Saturday."

"I should probably say the same thing to you." Robert looked as impeccable today as he had the day before. He held a cup of designer coffee in one hand and a newspaper in the other. "I had some paperwork to get caught up on. End of the month bills, et cetera."

The other man's gaze skimmed Jack from head to toe. The look of disdain in Walker's eyes didn't go unnoticed. Quite frankly, Jack didn't give a damn. He knew he looked rough after traveling the day before and working through the postcards all night.

So be it. He'd rather worry about a case than his appearance any day. At this point in his career as a homicide detective, Jack had come to accept the fact that most days his appearance wasn't much better than that of some of his victims.

Walker, on the other hand, appeared to be a man who put a high price on fashion and first impressions.

"We were out of cream, so I ran next door." Abby's voice filtered into the room several moments before she appeared. "I don't know about you, but after last night, I'm not settling for black coffee."

One of Robert's pale brows arched in the moment before he shifted his attention to Abby.

"Robert." She stuttered to a stop in the doorway. "I didn't realize you were working today."

"Just came in." He smiled, tucking his newspaper under one arm to reach for the box of doughnuts Abby juggled along with two foam coffee cups.

"Thanks."

An odd sensation rankled inside Jack's gut as he

watched Abby shift her load, transferring the box to Robert. Her features softened, her eyes brightened, and if he weren't mistaken, she and Robert shared a lightning-fast look reminiscent of the way Jack had seen lovers do.

Were Abby Conroy and Robert Walker more than business partners? Jack had seen no sign of that possibility at Abby's apartment other than the occasional photograph. And she'd mentioned nothing of the sort, not that she would. The woman struck him as anything but someone who shared her thoughts easily. Ironic, considering she spent her days hoping the public would confess en masse.

"Something going on I should know about?" Robert asked, never taking his gaze from Abby.

She nodded, but it was Jack who spoke.

"There was another postcard in yesterday's mail."

Robert's brows drew together as he frowned.

"I forgot to sort the cards." Abby gave a quick shrug as she handed Jack his coffee then set her cup on the table. "I went by the post office box on my way in, but once I stumbled upon you and Detective Grant, I never took the mail out of my pocket. I remembered them last night after Dwayne left…"

Her voice trailed off noticeably toward the end of her sentence and Jack noted the angry look that flashed across Robert's face.

Apparently Abby's partner wasn't a Dwayne fan, either, although he said nothing in response to Abby's statement.

"Did you call the authorities?" Robert asked.

Jack nodded, pursing his lips. "I'm working with local police, keeping them abreast of any developments. And I dusted for prints myself."

"And?" Robert's features tensed.

"And they agree with me that as of right now we have nothing to go on except the fact both cards bore no useable prints and were prepared using materials that could have been acquired anywhere."

"What about the photographs?" Robert asked.

"My thought—" Jack pulled the second postcard from his case file "—is that the photos used to make the postcards are scans of the originals."

"And you're some sort of photography expert?" Robert's brows lifted toward his too-neat hairline.

Jack shook his head, not even trying to hide his amusement at Walker's arrogance. "And you are?"

Walker shrugged. "I used to dabble. May I take a look?"

Jack handed the photo to Robert, studying the man as he stared intently at both sides of the card.

"I think you're right. The quality isn't that of a true photograph."

"More like a high-quality personal printer."

Robert nodded, continuing to scrutinize Emma's photograph, his expression revealing not a clue as to what he was thinking. "Pretty girl."

"She was." Jack fought the urge to put his fist through a wall, something he had only done once in his life—the day Boone Shaw walked free.

"One of your victims?" Robert's expression brightened.

"Yes." Jack gave a sharp nod. "And she's my sister."

Robert let loose a long, low whistle. "My sympathies." He turned over the card to reread the message, drawing in a sharp breath as if the words meant more now that he knew the victim was a relative. "When?"

"Same week as Melinda Simmons. Christmas week, eleven years ago."

Robert handed the card back to Jack. "Why confess now? Why use our site?"

Jack tucked the card back into the file without looking at Emma's full-of-life eyes captured in the photograph.

How long had she lived after that moment? What hell had she suffered at the hands of her killer?

"I'd imagine he saw your *People* magazine feature and decided you were the surest means to an end."

"An end?"

"His fifteen minutes of fame." Jack gathered up his notes, tucking the folder and his papers back into his brief-case. "For some reason he's decided now's the time to get the credit he deserves."

"I'm not following you." Robert narrowed his eyes.

"You'd be surprised how many psychopaths reach a point where they want to be caught," Jack replied.

A shadow crossed Robert's face, an emotional response Jack couldn't quite read.

"Isn't that a bit clichéd?" Robert asked.

"Perhaps." Jack forced a polite smile. "But true. These killers work so hard not to get caught that there's no noto-riety for them. Sometimes they crack. They want the at-tention they feel they deserve."

"The credit?" Robert repeated, as if weighing the word.

Jack nodded.

"Why now?"

"Maybe he's sick or feels he's running out of time. Maybe he feels threatened by a new killer. Maybe he's simply bored with being anonymous."

"Amazing." Robert smiled, the move not reaching his unreadable eyes. "Good work, Detective." Then he turned, heading toward the door. "Speaking of work, I'd better get to mine."

With that, Robert was gone, leaving Jack and Abby to their roomful of postcards.

"Not a warm and fuzzy fellow?" Jack asked after Robert was out of earshot.

"He doesn't like the cards." Abby handed Jack a cup of

coffee. "He probably broke into a cold sweat just being near this many."

Jack frowned.

"Says they give him the creeps," Abby continued.

"So why does he do this?"

She screwed up her features as if the answer were a no-brainer. "He does it to help me."

Jack said nothing, knowing from years of interrogation that sometimes silence was the fastest way to discover additional information. Abby didn't disappoint.

"He handles the business aspect and the promotion. I handle the postcards and write the weekly blog."

"And this keeps you both busy full-time?"

She shook her head. "I paint. Landscapes mainly. Murals. Robert does freelance marketing. Speeches. Brochures. Advertising design. Things like that."

"So you both work here all day then work at home each night."

Abby nodded. "More or less. We rarely put in full days here. This—" she gestured to the office in front of and behind her "—allows us flexibility to do our own things."

"You working on a mural right now?" Jack asked the question knowing it seemed unrelated to the case at hand, but realizing you never knew where the facts of a case might lead you.

But Abby only shook her head. "Last thing anyone wants at Christmas time is a mural painter in their home or office."

Jack scanned the stacks of cards filling the room. "Any income from this?"

"Only from the advertising. It's enough to cover hosting and office expenses, but not much more. We really didn't start this for the money, so that aspect doesn't matter to either one of us."

"Any enemies?"

His question visibly startled Abby and she took a backward step. "Not that I know of."

Jack pushed away from the table. "Then we keep our eyes and ears open until we know for sure who's on your side and who isn't. And in the meantime, let's go write that blog of yours."

JACK STOOD OVER Abby's shoulder as she worked, later than usual in drafting her weekly blog.

Typically, she tried to have the site updated just after midnight each Friday night. Considering it was now after noon on Saturday, she was running seriously behind schedule.

Robert had stayed less than forty-five minutes before he'd claimed to have forgotten a social event scheduled for that afternoon. Abby knew him well enough to know he hadn't planned on having company here at the office. He'd probably packed up the bills to take home for processing.

As for the blog, Abby had tucked away the cards she'd planned to feature, working instead from only one.

The postcard and photo featuring Emma Grant.

The young woman's smiling face haunted Abby. She couldn't begin to imagine the kind of hurt the image had brought to life deep inside Jack.

For all of his hard-shelled bravado, the detective's eyes provided a window into the pain he'd locked inside. Abby didn't need to be a rocket scientist to spot his true emotions, and she grimaced on his behalf.

She hadn't known him long, but she'd seen enough to know Jack wouldn't be pleased by her observation. Some men prided themselves on being strong, resilient, alpha males. Jack Grant fell soundly into that camp—the camp that said real men didn't show their feelings.

But as her gaze dropped again to Emma's face, and Abby considered the magnitude of the loss Jack had suffered, she didn't see how he could feel nothing, yet nothing was all he projected.

A man would have to be a robot to keep that sort of heartache locked inside forever. Sooner or later, he'd snap. Either that, or he'd shut down completely. How else could a person survive?

Jack stood behind her as she worked, the heat of his body warming the back of her sweater.

Well, the man definitely was not a robot.

Abby had never written one of her blogs with someone breathing down her neck, but she understood why the detective watched her every move, studied her every word. He'd made a commitment to clear a case, to catch a killer, to ease the suffering of the families left behind.

He was here because he thought Abby could help him. Plain and simple. He was here to make sure she didn't misstep in their efforts to flush out the postcard's sender.

She might be used to working alone, but Jack's goal had become her goal, and she'd do whatever it took to help him in his cause.

"Am I distracting you?" Jack asked, as if reading Abby's thoughts.

He leaned so close his breath brushed the strands of the hair she'd twisted up into a clip so that she could concentrate. In fact, she'd thought about the detective's proximity long enough that she'd begun to imagine the feel of his breath against the bare expanse of her throat.

What would the touch of his hand be like should he shift his grasp from the back of the chair to her shoulder?

A shudder rippled through her, coiling her belly into a tight knot. Heat ignited, low and heavy at her core.

What on earth was wrong with her?

She'd had no sleep, true. Perhaps she could use that to explain the unwanted thoughts about Jack Grant…and his hand…and the heat he inspired.

Abby's face warmed, making her thankful Jack stood where he couldn't see her sudden flush of embarrassment.

"Abby?"

"Yes?"

"I asked if I was distracting you, but based on the fact you didn't hear me, I'd have to say no."

If only he knew the truth.

She shook her head. "No. You're not distracting me at all."

And then she forced her thoughts back to the screen and the words she'd written, her admonition of a killer out to leave his mark on the public psyche by sending handmade postcards confessing his former sins.

Yet as much as she tried to deny it, the distraction of Jack's presence hung in the back of Abby's mind, a tiny voice refusing to be silenced, refusing to be ignored—even though that's exactly what Abby intended to do.

TENSION VIBRATED OFF of Abby Conroy, pulsating in waves. Jack had shattered her illusions of the world and the innocence of her postcard confession site, he knew that. But he wasn't sorry.

He'd done what he'd had to do, and if he had to expose Abby to the harsh reality of the world in order to unearth Boone Shaw, he would.

He had a job to do, and a killer to track down and trap.

"You're sure you don't mind me reading over your shoulder?" he asked again.

The woman answered with only a sharp shake of her head.

Jack leaned in closer, inhaling the lemony scent of whatever products she'd used on her hair the day before.

Fresh. The woman smelled fresh, even after the long night they'd shared.

Her fingers flew across the keyboard as she typed. Long, slender fingers, sure in their purpose. She leaned forward slightly. Moving away from his nearness? Or lost in her concentration?

He'd guess the latter, though the increasing tension arcing between them had grown palpable.

Too much time together in small spaces over long hours could do that to any two people. He should know.

He thought back to the cases he'd worked over the years. The women he'd met. He'd allowed himself brief involvements, but nothing more. His work didn't allow room for distraction of an emotional nature.

Then Jack pulled his thoughts back to this moment, this woman, *this* case.

His gaze drifted from the blog's words to Abby's face, lit by the monitor screen, her eyes bright, animated, determined. Her chin jutted forward as if nothing scared her, as if nothing could touch her. The protectiveness simmering deep inside Jack edged aside to allow another emotion to spring to life, uncoiling and spreading. Admiration? Attraction?

He shifted his stance, sliding his grip from the back of her chair to the arm by her side.

Abby's body stiffened, then immediately relaxed. She was more affected by his presence than she'd admitted.

Something tightened deep in his center. A need he'd long denied, a craving he'd vowed to never honor again.

"You think this works?"

Abby's voice filtered into his brain, her soft tone adding to thoughts of the case, his past, and Abby, swirling and battling for position.

What would it be like to hear that soft voice under different circumstances? Whispered in his ear? Against his neck? Lips feathering the bare skin of his chest?

"Good job." Jack cleared his throat and pushed back from her chair, hoping Abby hadn't heard the raspy quality of his voice. "I'd better be heading back to my hotel. I've got some work to do."

Lord knew he needed something to redirect his brain from thoughts of Abby back to thoughts of the case. Plus, he imagined the woman would be ready to head home once the blog was posted. Neither of them had slept since the night before.

Jack's last mistake had been getting involved with an associate on a case, a young district attorney who'd turned out to be playing for both sides.

While he didn't expect Abby to do anything to jeopardize his search for Shaw, he couldn't deny his thoughts had begun to border on distraction.

Jack hadn't been with a woman in a long, long time, and Abby Conroy was wreaking havoc on his senses.

But Jack was a man of conviction. A man of control. And he wasn't about to let lust get in the way of focus or justice. Not now.

Not ever.

Chapter Five

Jack had been gone for less than an hour when Abby heard the bell at the front of building signal a new arrival.

Even though she'd been happy with her blog entry calling out the postcard sender, she hadn't yet hit the publish button on her management program.

The bell sounded again and Abby sucked in a breath, held it and keyed in the steps to update the blog.

Then she pushed out of her chair, filled with a sense of anticipation, not knowing what the future would bring. For the sake of Jack Grant and the other victims' families, she hoped the postcards and blogs would lead the authorities to the killer, this time bringing him to justice and the cold case to closure.

She squinted as she headed toward the reception area, not recognizing the man who stood on the other side of the glass door.

Well-dressed and polished, she'd guess him to be in his late thirties based on the tinges of silver at his temples. He smiled as she approached and Abby found herself reminded of her partner Robert's smile at times. Too perfect. Too practiced.

Robert had spent years being a misfit during their

younger days and had used his smile to project a confidence he never felt.

Abby couldn't help but wonder what this stranger's excuse was.

"Can I help you?" She asked the question without unlocking the door.

She considered the Trolley Square area to be safe, but after Jack's comment that the postcard sender could be close by, she wasn't about to open the door to a stranger. Not when she was here alone.

"May I come in?" The man pressed a business card to the glass door as he spoke.

Sam Devine. Associated Press.

It looked like the killer's fifteen minutes of fame had just begun.

Abby unlocked the door, yet stood in the opening, not letting Mr. Devine any further into the building than necessary.

"I hope you won't mind my less than gracious welcome." Abby crossed her arms, hoping to make her message crystal clear. "I'm about to lock up, Mr. Devine. We're not open for business today."

"Your photo in the *People* article didn't do you justice."

Just what she needed. Hollow flattery. Abby plastered on a smile she in no way felt. "Can I help you, Mr. Devine?"

"Please—" he held out his hand and Abby gave it a quick shake "—call me Sam."

"Can I help you, Sam?"

"I received a tip about a second postcard."

Abby's heart caught. "A second postcard?"

Unless this man had somehow pulled up the Don't Say a Word site as he rang the bell, he'd have no way of knowing about the second card. Not to mention the fact his comment suggested he understood the significance of the first card, the photo of Melinda Simmons. Perhaps he'd spoken with Jack or the local police.

"Have you spoken to the police?"

Confusion slid across the reporter's features. "My tip wasn't from the police. It was from the killer."

Perhaps *Don't Say a Word* hadn't been the sender's sole target after all.

"You know about the Grant photo?" she asked.

Devine's eyes narrowed as he shook his head. "The Bricken photo."

"Bricken?" Abby didn't recognize the name from the articles she'd found regarding the New Mexico murders.

Devine's gaze brightened. "You're saying you received a card after the Simmons photo?"

So Jack Grant hadn't been the only one to recognize Melinda Simmons. How could Abby have published the postcard and called it a crank without digging deeper?

"You're familiar with the New Mexico case?" she asked.

Devine nodded, his features intent. "I studied it during my coverage of the local Bricken murder."

"*Beverly* Bricken?" Abby suddenly recognized the name and remembered the case.

The young woman had been a University of Delaware coed with everything to live for until someone had taken away all of her hopes and dreams by brutally ending her life five years earlier. Her body had been found shortly before Christmas, dumped in Valley Forge National Park.

The similarities between the Bricken case and Jack's case hit Abby like a sucker punch.

"When did you receive the Emma Grant postcard?" Devine asked.

Abby realized she might as well tell him. The information was public knowledge as of a few minutes ago. "Yesterday."

"Another message?"

She nodded. "She shouldn't have ignored me."

"Sonofagun."

Abby swallowed down a sudden knot in her throat. "You're saying the killer contacted you about the Bricken case?"

"Beverly Bricken," he repeated, stepping closer to where Abby stood. She instinctively took a matching step backward.

"What kind of tip?"

"E-mail."

"Did you trace his return address?"

Devine shook his head. "I tried after it came through my contact screen on the AP site, but our IT guys say it's untraceable."

But Abby was savvy enough to know there had to be a way to trace the contact. Her pulse quickened.

Beverly Bricken.

"Were you very involved in the investigation?" she asked, her mind spinning.

"Made my career." Another too-perfect smile. "Hey, what about your new postcard. May I see it?"

Abby pushed away from the reception desk. "It's in police custody."

Devine's face fell. The reporter had no doubt smelled an exclusive, as he did with the possibility of a third card.

"So, no Bricken card yet?" he asked.

"Not yet." But if this man were telling the truth, Abby would be receiving the new photo soon, if she hadn't already. She needed to check the site's post office box and fast.

"Have you retracted your statement about the Melinda Simmons card?"

Her statement, calling the killer a crank.

Abby nodded.

"I'd like to pursue the story, help draw this man out and bring him to justice. Would you let me do that, Ms. Conroy?"

Devine stepped close, too close, and suddenly Abby felt pinned in, her gut screaming a warning.

Something about the man was off.

"Do you have any other identification, Mr. Devine?"

"Sam." He reached into the inside pocket of his overcoat and Abby's stomach tightened.

She'd been beyond foolish to unlock the door based solely on a business card. Devine was more than likely harmless, but Abby needed Jack here with her, if for no other reason than to make sure she did or said nothing to jeopardize his work.

Devine held out his driver's license. Maryland.

The name matched the business card, but fake identification was bought and sold every day, wasn't it?

"I have another meeting, Sam," she bluffed, "but if you'd leave your card with me, I'll call you later. We can schedule a time to meet. I'd like you to meet the detective on the case. He was involved in the original investigation."

"Beverly Bricken's?"

"No." Abby handed back his license. "The New Mexico cases."

Devine's features fell, his disappointment evident. "The killer reached out to me, Ms. Conroy. You can trust me."

Sam Devine's words stopped Abby in her tracks, sending ice sliding through her veins. She'd always thought people who felt the need to say you could trust them frequently were unworthy of any trust at all.

Devine appeared anxious to claim this story as his own. He'd said the Bricken case made his career. Just how far would he go to relive that success? Had he seen the first blog, recognized Melinda Simmons and seized the opportunity to create a local angle?

"I'm not sure I'm ready to speak to the media just yet." Abby stepped toward Devine, hoping he'd take the hint and back toward the door. He sidestepped around her instead, moving past the reception desk, leaning against a pile of work to be sorted and filed.

"I'm more of a media consultant these days."

Abby moved quickly, stepping into Devine's path before he could move deeper into the building. Her pulse hummed in her ears.

"To-may-to, to-mah-to." Abby did her best to project a sense of bravado she in no way felt, wanting to keep the tone amicable yet move Devine out of the building. She pointed toward the front door. "I'll call you later to set up a meeting."

"So, you're refusing to comment?"

Now the man was putting words into her mouth. "I never said that. I assure you I'll comment later."

Sam Devine's friendly expression turned dark, almost menacing, and Abby realized she had no idea of what Boone Shaw looked like.

None of the articles she'd found online had included the former suspect's photograph, and Detective Grant hadn't yet provided that information to her.

For all she knew, the man standing within striking distance could be a cold-blooded killer posing as a consultant to the Associated Press.

Her insides tilted sideways.

Abby brushed past the reporter, pushing open the door to speed his exit.

Devine hesitated at the door, one hand on the jamb, a primal hunger flashing in his eyes. "I'll expect your call, Ms. Conroy."

The unease in Abby's belly tightened down into a knot. Surely she was overreacting, but Jack Grant had already accused her of being careless when it came to security.

Now was as good a time as any to change her ways.

She locked the door as soon as Devine was on the other side of the glass, not caring whether or not she'd offended the man.

She waited until he'd vanished from her sight, walking down the sidewalk and around the corner.

Closer than you think. Jack's words echoed in her brain.

The hair at the nape of Abby's neck pricked to attention.

Had someone given Sam Devine a tip? Or had he made up the story hoping to create a story where there hadn't yet been one?

Yet, if a third card existed, Jack would want to know about it right away. Abby's mind swirled with possibilities and questions, and she realized she needed Jack.

And she needed him now.

She reached for the phone tucked under the reception counter, knocking the pile of Natalie's work askew. She pulled Jack's card from her pocket and dialed, stretching to straighten up the mess she'd just made.

Natalie would have her head. The receptionist might be a sweetheart, but she took issue with anyone using—or messing up—her workspace.

Jack answered just as Abby's brain realized what she'd stumbled upon.

A black-and-white print. Tucked into Natalie's files.

She could make out pale hair, the curve of a feminine cheek, a slender neck.

For a split second, Abby's mind shut down, refusing to process what she was seeing.

A third postcard.

In the exact location where Sam Devine had just stood.

JACK TOOK A long swallow of weak coffee, grimaced then adjusted the screen on his laptop. He'd used his Phoenix police department identification to log in to his favorite database as soon as he'd gotten back to his hotel room.

The gray sky outside was threatening snow and he'd been in no mood to get swept up in the crush of holiday shoppers swarming the mall next to his hotel. Nor had he been in the mood to take a drive in the nearby countryside to clear his head.

He'd been in the mood to find Boone Shaw and know exactly what the man was up to. But Boone Shaw was gone, falling off the radar screen more than a month earlier. The man had left the antique shop and photography studio he ran behind, taking only one thing—his camera.

Jack ran a search on Shaw's known credit cards and came up with nothing. Not a single hit during the past six weeks. The man was nothing if not smart, and if he had traveled from Montana to Delaware, he'd done so using cash. Anything else would have been flagged by the system.

Cash, on the other hand, would allow Shaw to become a ghost—untraceable in a society that had become a master of tracing the movements of its citizens.

Jack attempted another drink of the weak coffee, then pushed away from the desk, carrying the coffee cup toward the bathroom sink. He dumped the contents down the drain, then tossed the cup into the waste bin. He caught his reflection out of the corner of his eye and stopped cold.

His five o'clock shadow was apparently working over-time. Jack scrubbed a hand over his jaw, and cranked open the spigot. He'd learned a long time ago that a shower and shave did wonders for a man's thinking.

Ten minutes later, he stood in front of the same mirror,

towel anchored around his waist, beads of moisture glistening on his shoulders and chest.

And then it hit him. The certain something that had been nagging at him all day.

Robert Walker.

Jack didn't like the man, and he couldn't figure out why.

Was it because the man and Abby were so close they shared the same unspoken language? Did Jack envy Robert the relationship?

"Snap out of it," Jack said to his reflection.

Abby Conroy was a beautiful woman, and her secret confession site was most likely the key to finding Boone Shaw. Nothing more.

But Robert Walker. Something about the man ate at Jack, but what?

He had no reason to suspect him of anything other than being a know-it-all, but what could it hurt to have a bit more information?

Jack settled in front of the laptop once more, this time keying in Robert Walker's name. Jack pulled first the man's home address and driver's license information, then worked backward, accessing previous tax information, addresses and employer records.

Walker had spent his years in Delaware, at least since he'd graduated from the University of Delaware. He'd also devoted his career to the computer industry, so working on the Don't Say a Word site hadn't been a stretch.

He'd attended high school and grade school locally and by all appearances was a loyal native who had never done so much as miss a day of school. So why did he make the tiny alarm bells in Jack's brain clang to attention?

Simple.

Abby Conroy.

Much as Jack hated to admit it, the woman had thrown his typically astute judge of character off-kilter.

He was just about to give himself a sound mental thrashing when his cell rang.

He'd put a call in to a buddy who specialized in private investigation; with any luck at all, the guy had made contact with Boone Shaw's wife.

"Yeah." Jack spoke even as he did his best to shove all inappropriate thoughts of Abby Conroy out of his mind, yet it was Abby whose voice filtered across the line.

"I found another card."

He was on his feet, dropping the towel from his waist and pulling a clean pair of jeans from his bag before she could say another word. "You're still at the office?"

"Yes."

"Was it in the mail?"

Silence beat across the line.

"Abby?" Damn, but he should have never left her alone.

"Front desk."

How in the hell? He buttoned his jeans and dug around in his bag for a shirt. "The reception desk?" Jack balanced the phone on one side of his neck and then the other as he shrugged into a well-worn denim shirt, fastening the buttons as he searched for his shoes.

"Yes."

"Don't touch anything and lock those damned doors. I'm on my way."

"Jack?"

"Yeah." He grabbed his coat from the bed and headed for his hotel room's door.

"A reporter came to see me."

"And?"

"He said he'd received a tip."

A tip? "From where?"

"The killer."

Jack squeezed his eyes shut momentarily. If there was one thing he hated, it was the press.

"What was the reporter's name?"

"Sam Devine."

Jack made a mental note. He'd be calling Detective Tim Hayes the second he disconnected from Abby. "You found the new card after Devine left?"

Abby's sharp intake of air was all the answer Jack needed.

"I'll be there in ten minutes."

If he hurried, he could make it in five.

Chapter Six

Jack pounded on the locked glass door six minutes later. Without thinking, he grasped Abby's shoulders the moment she opened the door, meeting her frightened eyes and wanting to turn back time so that he could have been with her when she found the card.

"What does he look like?" she asked, her question pouring out in a monosyllabic slur of words.

"Who?"

"Shaw."

"Early fifties by now, bald, big and burly."

She blew out a sigh. "This wasn't him, then."

Jack furrowed his brow.

"The reporter," Abby explained. "Sam Devine. For one crazy moment, I thought he might be Shaw pretending to be a reporter." She shook her head. "You probably think I sound hysterical."

Abby turned to break away from him, but Jack tightened his hold on her shoulders, forcing her focus to his.

"I think you finally sound smart." Their gazes locked and held. "Boone Shaw is no one you want to mess around with, and neither is anyone who might be working with him."

Abby said nothing, but she also didn't move away. She

stood her ground, meeting Jack's stare. Her eyes searched his, until he broke contact, suddenly unable to stand close to the woman and think clearly at the same time.

"Tell me exactly what happened."

Abby recounted the exchange, ending with her discovery of the card during the moments she waited for Jack to answer the phone.

"Were you watching him the entire time?"

She nodded, her pale eyes huge with the shock of the day's events.

"Do you think he could have planted the card?" Jack asked.

"I would have seen him, but you have to admit the timing is a bit tough to overlook."

Jack couldn't agree more. "I already put in a call to Hayes."

He slipped on a pair of thin gloves as he spoke, preparing to lift the card from the stack of files. "He knows Devine, vouched for him actually, although he said the guy was more than a little obsessed with a local murder victim, Beverly Bricken."

Abby reached for Jack's arm, her touch heating the skin beneath his shirt. "Devine said that was who the third postcard would be based on his tip."

Jack frowned. Maybe Boone Shaw wasn't behind the postcards after all. Was it possible?

"Could she have been killed by the same guy?" Abby asked.

The question stopped Jack in his tracks. "If there were any similarities, the national database would have triggered a call to me."

His voice trailed off as he studied the young woman's image captured on the card. She was physically different from the New Mexico victims, as blonde as they'd been brunette. Her face was fuller, her makeup heavier, yet she'd been posed similarly, as if the shot had been intended for submission to a modeling agency.

"Would you recognize this Beverly Bricken?" he asked.

Abby's throat worked. "That's her."

"You're sure?"

"I'm an artist, Jack. I remember details."

He turned over the card and read aloud. "No one likes a show off."

When he looked up at Abby this time, the color had drained from her cheeks. The episode had shaken her badly and he needed to get her away from here.

He also needed to get in touch with Sam Devine. He had a few questions for the man.

Perhaps there was a way to kill two birds with one stone.

"Did he leave a contact number?"

"Devine?"

Jack nodded and Abby reached into her pocket, stepping toward Jack to hand over the card she'd extracted.

Jack kept his focus on Abby as she moved, measuring her body language and the set of her features.

Even though her coloring reflected her fragile state, she hadn't relaxed the proud set of her shoulders, nor had she surrendered the stubborn line of her jaw. Her eyes, however, reflected the slightest glimmer of fear.

Much as he wanted to erase that fear and the sense of vulnerability he'd put there with his harsh words about her safety, Jack had a killer to put away before the man began to do more than deliver postcards.

Priorities were priorities and right now Jack needed to know how much Sam Devine knew about Boone Shaw, Beverly Bricken and the postcard now resting on top of the receptionist's desk.

He also needed to know whether or not Devine had planted the newest postcard.

If not Devine, he didn't want to consider the fact the killer might have been as close to Abby as this reception desk.

"Has anyone else been here today since I left?"

Abby shook her head. "No one since Robert stopped by this morning."

Robert.

Jack flashed on the image of Abby's partner as he'd arrived earlier that day. Hell, the man could have hidden a fistful of postcards in the newspaper he'd carried.

The bottom line was that the third postcard had been hand-delivered. The question now was, by whom?

Jack studied Devine's business card then did his best to give Abby a reassuring smile.

"What do you say we see what your new friend Sam Devine is doing for dinner?"

SAM DEVINE EAGERLY agreed to meet Jack and Abby at the Concord Mall food court later that evening.

In the meantime, Jack followed Abby home and waited outside her apartment until her friend Gina arrived to keep her company. Based on Gina Grasso's take-no-prisoners appearance, Jack had the feeling Abby was in good hands for the time being.

Then Jack headed straight to the local precinct. Judging from the skeptical look on Tim Hayes's face, the man was as wary of Sam Devine's sudden appearance as Jack was.

"So you're saying he claims the sender sent him an e-mail?" Hayes asked.

"An untraceable e-mail through a contact form on the Associated Press Web site."

"And you believe that?"

"No."

Detective Tim Hayes squeezed his eyes shut momentarily and pinched the bridge of his nose. "I'll have my guys check that out."

It was obvious the man felt lousy, his voice scratchy and his eyes shot with red.

Jack apparently wasn't the only one who could live without experiencing a cold, white Christmas. Give him a cactus and a Santa cap any day and he'd be content. Actually, he could skip the Santa cap.

"You said you knew him?" Jack asked, leaning forward across the break room table.

Each man nursed a high-test cup of coffee. It was no wonder most officers' stomachs rotted out by the time they earned their pensions, if not sooner.

The two men had settled in the precinct's break room, blissfully quiet at this time on a late Saturday afternoon. The calm before the storm of a Saturday night, Jack imagined.

"I remember the name from the Bricken case." Hayes studied the postcard through clear plastic, grimacing. "If he's the guy I think he is, he was a pain in the ass. Always wanting the latest and greatest news on the case before we held press conferences. His coverage made him a local celebrity for a short time."

Hayes shook his head. "I'll be honest. I haven't heard his name or seen his byline in a long time. I'd forgotten the man existed."

Exactly the sort of reporter to seize the postcard scenario as an opportunity to create a renewed purpose... and fame.

"You think he made this himself?" Hayes asked, looking from the card to Jack then back to the card again.

"It's crossed my mind."

Hayes nodded. "That would be my first thought. Unless your killer spent some time in Delaware five years ago and we never matched up the pieces."

Jack shrugged, knowing Hayes's theory could be a possibility. "Were there other victims at the time?"

Hayes drew in a breath, coughed, then sat back against the metal chair, the legs of the chair scraping against the battered linoleum floor.

"Just the one. Beverly Bricken. She went missing the week before Christmas."

Jack recognized the frustration in the other man's grimace. Call it the curse of a homicide detective who cared, call it whatever you want.

Good detectives never forgot the cases they didn't clear or the families to whom they never gave closure.

And if they were good at what they did, some small part of their brain never stopped working the cold cases—Jack thought of Emma, laughing and alive—as much as they tried.

"Her body was found in Valley Forge Park three days later, by a family out for a walk. Dog was off the leash. He veered off the trail and never looked back once he got the scent."

"Cause of death?" Jack slid the stack of crime scene photos from in front of Hayes, turning them to face him.

"Ligature marks at the neck indicated strangulation," Hayes said flatly, without emotion. Another telltale sign of a homicide detective who had learned to shut down his own humanity in order to relate the cold, harsh facts of a case without losing his sanity.

"Same as my guy." Jack's hand settled on a photo of Beverly Bricken's face, still beautiful, even in death. "Sexual assault?"

Hayes nodded. "This was not a nice guy."

"None of them are."

"You had five dead in one spree?" Hayes asked, leaning forward again, the alert edge returning to his voice.

"Only four bodies." Jack flashed again on the day Shaw had walked free. He remembered the anguished faces of Mr. and Mrs. Simmons as they realized their daughter's killer had just gone free. "Melinda Simmons was never found."

"But you included her in the case?"

"Her photos were part of what we took from Shaw's studio. Her personal effects were found in the desert."

"Animals?" Hayes spoke the word softly for being such a big man.

"Coyotes more than likely." Jack narrowed his gaze. "They'd gotten to some of the other victims, as well, but we'd still been able to make IDs."

"But not with the Simmons girl?"

Jack shook his head, the uninvited memory of Herb Simmons's voice echoing in his brain.

Don't let him get away this time.

"So you had no way of knowing whether or not she was marked like your other victims?"

Marked.

Detective Hayes had done his homework.

A crude eye had been drawn onto each New Mexico victim's upper thigh by what investigators had theorized was some sort of branding tool, similar to those used by artisans to engrave leather.

They'd never matched the wounds to anything found in Boone Shaw's possession. Another piece that hadn't helped the prosecution's case.

"I see you know a bit about my case." Jack flipped to the next photo in the stack.

"It's not every day a detective from Arizona shows up

in Wilmington, Delaware, hoping to find his man for a series of murders in New Mexico."

But Jack barely heard Hayes's words. His focus had locked on the subject of the photo before him.

Beverly Bricken's body bore some sort of symbol on the flesh of her upper thigh, the spot identical to where the New Mexico victims had been marked.

Jack tapped the photograph. "Did you release this nationally?"

He'd flagged the interstate database to alert him if so much as one other murder or assault victim were branded by their attacker, as his victims had been.

He'd never had a hit that matched or came close. He'd also never heard of Beverly Bricken before today, yet there she was. Branded.

"We kept it quiet for a while," Hayes said. "Never let the media get a hold of it. When we did put it in the system, nothing came back."

"That doesn't make sense. Every single one of my cases is in there." Jack caught himself. "At least the four victims we were sure about." He looked more closely at the photo. "What is that?"

"Looks like her killer cut it into her skin," Hayes answered. "A pair of lips as best we can tell. Sick idea of a signature."

"Lips," Jack muttered. Then the ramification of the rest of Hayes's statement hit him. Jack set down the photo and winced. He'd been looking for other victims branded with an eye. Branded. If the Wilmington investigation had deemed their marking to be a pair of lips cut into the victim, no wonder the database had never connected the dots.

"Any chance that's burned into her skin?" Jack asked, angling the photo toward Hayes.

"Burned?"

"Branded into her flesh."

"Anything's possible," Hayes said flatly.

Jack pushed to his feet and scrubbed a hand across his face. "This guy's not wired like we're wired. He wants the control. What better way to communicate you're in charge than to brand your victims?"

"Like cattle."

"Like cattle," Jack repeated.

Hayes straightened from his chair and stepped into Jack's path. "You think this is your guy?"

Jack thought long and hard before he answered. Same MO. Similar signature. Young coed killed in the prime of her life, her body dumped in a nearby national park. "Too many similarities to ignore."

"Maybe my guy read about your case, decided to try it for himself. Maybe that explains the similarities."

Hayes had a point. "True. Or maybe my guy decided to mix it up a bit in a new location."

"After a six-year hiatus?" Hayes frowned.

"All depends on the trigger." Jack flipped through the file, not finding what he wanted. "What about trace evidence on the body? Hair? Fiber?"

"Nothing." Hayes shook his head. "A careful and cruel killer."

"Same here."

"If it's the same killer, why wait until the third card to reach out to Devine?" Hayes asked.

Jack pressed his lips together before he spoke. "Local case. Local contact. As long as whoever killed Bricken stuck around long enough, he'd have witnessed Devine's obsession with the case. Maybe he wasn't happy with the reaction he got from Abby.

"Or maybe Devine saw the connection none of us had

spotted before," Jack continued. "Maybe he saw the first postcard as his opportunity to resurrect the case."

"Or his career," Hayes added.

"No arguments there."

"What about your original suspect, Boone Shaw?"

"He fell off the radar screen several weeks back," Jack explained. "I've got someone working on finding his trail. I'll have him check out Shaw's whereabouts at the time Bricken was murdered. Make sure he didn't take any cross-country trips."

"In the meantime, we've got to figure out how deep Devine's involvement goes." Hayes lifted the encased postcard from the table. "I'll walk this to the lab myself."

"With any luck at all, we'll figure this mess out before our guy strikes again."

"As long as he sticks to postcards, we're all right." Hayes smiled grimly.

Hayes was right. One postcard might be the work of a man seeking public acknowledgment of his work. Two postcards was the work of a man who was either pissed off about Abby's first blog or who wanted broader media coverage.

Three cards, potentially linking cases years and miles apart, was a message from the killer that he'd shifted tacks once before, and was more than capable of doing so again.

Assuming, of course, that the third card came from the same source as the first two. An assumption Jack wasn't ready to make. On the other hand, he couldn't afford to dismiss the possibility.

Abby's beautiful face flashed through Jack's mind, his gut tightening with an unforgiving twist as he echoed the other detective's words. "Let's hope he sticks to postcards."

ABBY WILLED HER temples to stop pounding as she and Jack headed toward their meeting with Devine. It was bad enough that Gina had all but thrown herself at Jack the moment they'd met, but she'd also thrown herself at Dwayne…for far different reasons.

Abby's neighbor had handed over the mail he'd taken earlier that day from her private mailbox. Unfortunately, he'd done so in front of Gina, who had gone ballistic, accusing Dwayne of everything from mail theft to identity fraud to stalking.

Abby groaned at the memory then held her head.

"You all right?"

"Nothing a little food won't cure."

Food…and some answers.

According to what Jack had found out during his meeting with Detective Hayes, Devine had gone from hero to zero after the Beverly Bricken case grew cold.

Experience in the art world had taught Abby that some people would do most anything to return to the limelight once they'd had a taste of success in their chosen field.

She couldn't help but wonder whether or not Devine was one of those people, and if so, how far would he go to regain his public persona?

Would he plant evidence? Copycat a killer's postcard? Fabricate a phantom e-mail?

The local police, working with the Web master for the AP site, had confirmed Devine had not received the e-mail in question.

Abby couldn't wait to see how fast Devine's smile crumbled once Jack hit him with that fact.

"What's our objective here?" she asked.

An uncharacteristic grin pulled at the corner of Jack's mouth. Abby rankled. The man considered her nothing more than an amateur.

"Your objective is to sit quietly and let me work," he answered.

Abby shot a look out the passenger window then turned her now volatile combination of fear and impatience on Jack.

"Why am I going with you if you consider me such a liability?"

Jack's grin widened, warming the sharp lines of his profile. "My reasoning is simple." He smiled, enjoying whatever it was he was about to say. "I don't know what Devine looks like."

Abby laughed, the sound more a tired burst of air than anything else. "That's why I'm included?"

"Take it or leave it."

She had no intention of missing this meeting. "I'll take it."

Fifteen minutes later, she'd located Devine, sitting alone at a table intended for four. Devine, however, had removed one chair and shoved it alongside the next table over, as if he needed the assurance no surprise guest would sit in on their meeting.

"There." She pointed quickly, dropping her arm back to her side before she drew attention.

A matter of moments later, the necessary introductions had been made and Sam Devine had started talking.

Jack had dealt with a lot of reporters in his day, but he'd never encountered one so passionate about a case.

Excitement danced in Sam Devine's eyes. He wanted this too much.

More than a reporter out for a story.

More than a curious brain at work.

The Beverly Bricken case was personal for Sam Devine. The question was, why?

"Did you bring the postcards?" Excitement dripped from the reporter's words.

Jack shook his head and Devine's eager smile slipped.

The reporter reached up to brush a lock of hair from his forehead. A nervous tell, Jack decided. Something to take note of.

"I was looking forward to seeing them in person."

"And reliving your past success?" Jack asked.

Jack knew from talking to Hayes that Devine had been obsessed with the case. How far would he go now to solve it? Or to recreate his time in the spotlight?

"The Bricken case was a big part of my career, I'm not going to deny that. But the Christmas Confessor reached out to me and me alone. I deserve to be in the loop here."

"No, you don't," Jack said sharply.

"Why did you just call him the Christmas Confessor?" Abby asked, taking the words out of Jack's mouth.

Much as he agreed with her line of questioning, Jack shot Abby a warning glare and she fell silent once again.

Devine tipped his chin proudly. "Perfect timing, don't you think? Nothing the public loves more than the holidays and having a name for their serial killers."

No wonder this guy had fallen from grace.

"We don't know that this is a serial killer." Jack shook his head, enjoying the disappointment plastered across Devine's face. "For all we know, it's some kid sending in photos he found in a Dumpster somewhere."

Jack had learned long ago that some reporters were so hungry for a headline it made no difference who they trampled on their way to the top. "Someone who wants to spin the news, if you will," he continued.

Devine blanched and Jack knew he'd hit the mark. The reporter knew far more about the arrival of the third card than he was letting on.

Jack decided to cut to the chase.

"Did you plant the card in the Don't Say a Word office?"

Devine straightened defensively. "Detective, I am a

newsman, and a newsman does not fabricate a story. He reports the news."

"In an ideal world." Jack took a bite of the sandwich he'd snagged from one of the fast-food counters framing the seating area. He let Devine stew a bit while he chewed then swallowed. "In an ideal world, a reporter doesn't make up a bogus e-mail tip."

He studied Devine's shocked expression. The reporter had underestimated the speed with which the local police would blow his story sky-high.

"We know you lied." Jack pursed his lips and nodded. "There never was an e-mail."

"Perhaps I just know how to protect my source."

Jack arched a brow. "A murderer? You'd protect a murderer?"

Devine said nothing, although hot color blazed to life in his cheeks.

"In an ideal world," Jack continued. "A third murder victim's photograph—a murder never before connected to the other two—does not appear within minutes of a reporter's uninvited arrival, tucked between files on the very desk beside which that same reporter stood."

Devine remained silent, exactly the reaction Jack had anticipated.

Jack leaned back in his seat and blew out a sigh. "There's one other piece of this puzzle that confuses me, Mr. Devine. Maybe you can help me out here. Why do you suppose your *source* would wait until the third card to reach out?"

Devine blinked, pushing away his food tray. His complexion had gone splotchy beneath the unforgiving lighting inside the food court. "Maybe he felt he wasn't getting enough attention from Ms. Conroy's blog."

Much to Abby's credit, she said nothing, sitting back and soaking in every word, just as Jack had requested.

After the reporter declared Jack's investigational skills incompetent and stormed off, Jack turned to Abby, offering her one of his fries.

"What's your take?"

"He's lying." Abby's gaze widened before she bit into the fry. "Flat-out lying."

Jack turned to study Devine's hastily retreating figure. "There never was a tip."

"How do you explain the Bricken card?" Abby dropped her voice to a whisper.

"I think he pasted it together himself." Jack finished the last of his food and stuffed the leftover wrappers back into the restaurant bag. "He either wants the spotlight, or he wants to tie the two cases together."

"Maybe he wants both." Abby shrugged. "So where does that leave us?"

The fear Jack had spotted in Abby's expression earlier that day had eased a notch. Jack was glad, but he also didn't want her letting down her guard prematurely.

The real killer was out there somewhere, and until they found him, Jack couldn't risk leaving Abby alone again.

He pushed to his feet and held out a hand, savoring the touch of her slender fingers as she let him help her to her feet.

"It leaves me sleeping on your couch," Jack answered. "Until we know what in the hell is going on, I'm not leaving your side."

Chapter Seven

Abby was tired and chilled to the bone by the time she and Jack reached her apartment. The fresh wave of fear she'd experienced after finding the third card had eased, Jack's presence by her side infusing her with a sense of calm and security.

She'd noticed him stealing glances at her on the drive home and attributed the detective's attention to nothing more than the man doing his job—acting as protector.

Abby, however, found her head filled increasingly with thoughts of Jack Grant not purely as a detective, but also as a man.

He'd handled Sam Devine with such finesse he'd left Abby close to speechless, something not easy to do, if she admitted so herself.

On the drive back into town he'd called a private investigator named Max, asking the man to add a full background check for Sam Devine to his work, as well as checking Boone Shaw's whereabouts during the time Beverly Bricken had been murdered.

Jack had vowed to leave no stone unturned, and based on what Abby had seen, he was doing just that.

The curtains next door shifted as she and Jack covered the ground between Jack's car and the entry to her apartment. She almost lifted her hand to wave, when Jack gripped her elbow and hurried her along the sidewalk.

"He watches every move you make. You've got to stop encouraging him."

"He's harmless," she'd whispered, although a thread of anxiety wound its way through her at the intensity of Jack's words.

Now, a short while later, she found herself staring at the framed photo of Gina, Vicki and herself. It was Vicki's face in particular from which Abby couldn't wrench her focus.

She couldn't stop thinking about how Vicki's suicide had somehow set everything into motion. The birth of Don't Say a Word, the focus of a killer, postcards of young victims, their lives ended before they could begin.

Abby lost herself in her friend's image as if the truth lay hidden somewhere in the nuances of Vicki's features, clues left behind and captured on film.

She was being irrational, illogical, and she knew it. But she was tired and her sense of security and reality had been tilted on its axis.

Abby had surprised herself by letting Jack accompany her home. Normally, she rebelled against doing anything someone told her to do, but the shock of the past two days were enough to make even Abby realize she might not always know what was best.

If the detective thought she was safer with him inside her home, so be it.

Abby sat across from him now, watching the man stare down into a steaming mug of hot chocolate. The juxta-position of floating mini marshmallows and the man's tough exterior were enough to make her wish *she* had a camera.

Her gaze flickered again to Vicki's framed image.

"Do you want to tell me about it?"

"About what?" Abby let the steaming cup of hot chocolate she held warm her hands. The heat helped take the edge off the chill Devine's visit and today's postcard discovery had imprinted on every inch of her body.

Jack merely widened his gaze, the look saying he'd caught her staring again at the picture—the shot of Abby, Gina and Vicki, happy and smiling.

Abby had thought the detective engrossed by his own thoughts, but apparently he'd been watching Abby the entire time.

The intimate nature of Jack's question surprised Abby more than seeing the detective drink hot chocolate ever could.

"Do you really want to know?" Abby spoke without lifting her gaze to Jack's, without risking the way her heart had begun to catch each time their eyes met.

Tired. She was tired. Her defenses were weak. She kept telling herself that she and Jack Grant had been tossed into surreal circumstances. Take away the risk and the danger, and the attraction she felt would undoubtedly evaporate. She was sure of it.

She avoided his eyes, just the same.

"When was it taken?" he asked.

"Robert took it a few years ago at the unveiling of one of my murals." She pointed at the frame. "That's Gina and our friend Vicki. We've known each other—" she caught herself "—knew each other, since first grade."

"The three musketeers," Jack said with a slight smile.

The move softened the hard lines of his face, crinkling the skin around his dark eyes. Abby couldn't help but wonder how long it had been since the man smiled fully with abandon. Even now he held back, as if he'd decided long ago to disallow himself happiness.

Abby understood the feeling, understood the pain. She

stared again at the photo, remembering the night, the laughter, the friendship.

"We were the four musketeers, actually," she explained. "With the exception of the year after Robert's father died, we've been together since grade school."

"Any romantic involvement there?" Jack asked.

Defensiveness rippled through Abby. "Why is it people find it so difficult to believe men and women can be friends?"

Her sharp tone wiped all traces of Jack's smile from his face.

He set down his cup and leaned forward, elbows on knees. "I want to know how Don't Say a Word helps. Why did your friend's death compel you to reach out in such a public way?"

So Jack Grant knew about Vicki. The realization shouldn't surprise Abby. The detective had surely done his research before he'd traveled east. Hell, anyone who'd read the *People* magazine article would know about Vicki.

Was it the article that had drawn the attention of whoever was sending the postcards?

Abby dropped her focus from Vicki's picture, unable to meet her late friend's laughing eyes. "I could have been a better friend, Detective. I could have listened more."

"And you think that would have saved her?"

His voice held a note Abby hadn't heard there before. Concern. Perhaps there was far more heart hidden beneath the man's brawny physique than she'd imagined.

"I think it could have," Abby answered. Yet even as she spoke the words, she felt small and naive.

Once Vicki had decided to take her life, chances were nothing Abby might have said or done would have dissuaded her. At least, that's what the so-called experts had told Abby in an effort to ease her anguish in the days after Vicki's senseless death.

"We never found a note," Abby continued. "That's always bothered me."

"You doubt her death was suicide?" Jack's voice tightened.

"No." Abby set down her cup of hot chocolate and met Jack's stare. The intensity of his dark eyes momentarily stole her breath. "It makes me sad that even in that moment, in the seconds before she ended her life, she felt she had no one to talk to, not even in a suicide note."

"So you decided to give the public a forum?"

"For confessions." Abby pulled up her knees and wrapped her arms around her legs, settling back into the chair.

"To help them or to ease your guilt?"

Jack's words hit Abby like a slap. "So much for you being nonjudgmental."

His lips lifted in another subtle smile. "Who ever said anything about being nonjudgmental?"

Abby pushed out of her chair, suddenly tired of Jack's company and ready to be alone. She'd changed her mind about tonight. "Maybe your staying here isn't such a great idea."

But Jack didn't move. In fact, he settled further into the sofa, smoothing the cushions and readjusting the throwback pillows.

"I'm not going back to my hotel tonight, and you're not staying here alone."

"Well, I don't remember issuing an invitation for you to stay in the first place."

"You didn't. I made the decision all on my own."

Abby moved toward the door. "I'm happy for you, Detective, but I don't need you here. I want to be alone."

"Until we know how the Beverly Bricken postcard got inside your office, I'm not going anywhere."

Inside your office.

Jack's words stung, breaking loose the flood of anxiety Abby had worked so carefully to keep at bay.

She swallowed, struggling to maintain composure when she was so tired she could barely stand.

"Fair enough." She pointed to the hall leading back to her bedroom. "There's a guest bath and a linen closet that way. I'm sure there are plenty of leftovers in the fridge if you get hungry."

"You're going to give in, just like that?"

Abby couldn't help but laugh. This guy was one serious piece of work. "Just like that," she answered. "It's been a long two days. Good night, Detective."

"Sleep tight, Abby."

That had been two hours ago, and now here she stood, watching Jack Grant sleep.

Sleep tight.

She'd been on her way to the kitchen to grab a cup of water when she'd stopped to study the man.

Jack slept soundly on the sofa, his hand draped across a sheaf of papers. Even in sleep, his features reflected the tension of the day, the magnitude of the unknown they were facing.

She reached for a fleece throw and pulled it up over his legs, not wanting to disturb him and yet longing to touch his cheek. She shoved the crazy thought from her brain. Obviously, she'd better get some sleep herself. She'd begun to lose control of what little rationality she had left.

Jack's words rang through her mind as she watched him sleep.

Inside your office.

A shudder raced across her shoulders and down her spine.

The third postcard hadn't just been mailed to the

site's post office box, it had been placed inside her office. What next?

"You all right?" The rumble of Jack's tired voice jolted Abby from her thoughts. She hadn't realized he'd awakened; yet there he lay, watching her.

She nodded. "Just thirsty."

Jack narrowed his gaze and gave a quick shake of his head. "Thirsty doesn't put a look that worried on a face as beautiful as yours."

Now she was imagining things. There was no way Jack Grant had called her beautiful. Abby's traitorous stomach caught and twisted just the same.

"Abby?" Jack pulled himself to a sitting position and patted the sofa beside him.

"You were right," she said.

"I usually am."

"And humble." Abby warmed inside, enjoying their banter yet understanding the only reasons the mood had turned intimate were the late hour and their combined fatigue.

"I have a gift for reading people."

Abby wasn't about to argue—she'd seen him in action.

"So Don't Say a Word is more about your guilt than about helping others?"

She flinched, then moved to sit beside him on the sofa, keeping a respectable distance between them. "I wouldn't say that, though I do think it's helped the postcard confessors more than it's helped me."

He studied her, and she read his thoughts as if they were stamped on his forehead. Jack Grant saw right though her. His next statement confirmed the point.

"I've dealt with a lot of suicides during my time on the force. I know how difficult the situation can be for those left behind—"

"The situation?" His word choice left Abby cold.

"You probably think you neglected your friend in some way. You think you could have done more, listened more." He gave a slight lift and drop of his shoulders. "You think you should have seen her pain in time to stop her."

Abby had seen Vicki's pain, but she'd never guessed her oldest friend would take her life. How wrong she'd been.

And she wasn't about to tell Jack that not only had she stopped listening, she'd started avoiding, no doubt adding to Vicki's sense of despair.

"What about you? Do you think placing someone behind bars will help you put Emma's death behind you?"

He sank back against the sofa cushions, saying nothing for a moment. "It sounds straightforward when you say it like that, but I'll never put Emma's death behind me. I don't see how it's possible."

Abby glanced again at Vicki's framed image, the smooth glass obscuring details in the dim lighting. "I pick up the phone to call her at least once a day. I can't seem to make my subconscious realize she's gone."

She realized then that someone had replaced the broken glass. Gina, perhaps? She must have come back while Jack and Abby were with Devine.

"You didn't do anything wrong, Abby." Jack touched her knee lightly, sending a jolt of awareness through Abby's system.

He broke contact, but they remained where they were, both motionless.

"I won't let anything happen to you."

Jack's abrupt change of topic took Abby by surprise, but she realized in that moment that she trusted him, believed him, as if she'd known him for years.

The thought scared her to death. She hadn't trusted anyone in a very long time, and surely not with her life. Just the same, she realized she didn't want Jack to go back to his hotel in the morning. She wanted him by her side.

"I'd better get that water and let you get some sleep." She pushed to her feet and forced herself to look anywhere but into the detective's sleep-softened eyes.

Abby hugged herself, rubbing her upper arms as she turned once again for the kitchen.

The silhouette of something the size of a postcard, taped to the kitchen window, snapped her out of her protective cocoon in one fell swoop.

She leaned close to read the message on the card, flipping on the overhead kitchen light to better illuminate the simple black type.

It's time to stop living in the past.

Abby's blood ran cold.

"Jack."

He was at her side in a single beat of her heart, following the line of her gaze.

"Sonofa—" He spun away from her, racing for the front door. "Don't move."

Don't move. As if she could pull so much as a toe from the virtual concrete the postcard had set around her feet.

Jack reappeared outside, careful not to move too close to the window, yet scowling as he studied the image on the other side.

Another victim? Local? Or from New Mexico?

Based on the look on Jack's face, the photograph was of one of his victims. The anger flashing across his features went deep, too deep to have been a victim he didn't know.

He pulled his cell phone from his pocket and dialed, speaking quickly. Abby did her best to read his lips through the insulated glass, but failed miserably.

By the time he stepped back inside, the far-off wail of sirens could be heard, drawing steadily closer.

"Who did you call?" Abby asked the question without turning around, unable to rip her gaze from the postcard.

Jack's hands closed over her shoulders and squeezed, pulling her to him, her back to his chest. She longed to relax into his reassuring strength, longed to feel his arms reach around to hold her tight.

She longed to wake up tomorrow to find out tonight had been nothing more than a bad dream.

"Detective Hayes. Police are on their way."

The sirens outside intensified, closer now.

Abby asked the inevitable. "Who is it?"

"On the picture?"

She nodded.

Jack turned her to face him, shifting his hands to maintain contact, holding her as if he expected her to topple over at any moment. His expression had gone unreadable, a mixture of anger and determination and...*attraction?*

"Jack?"

His mouth opened and shut once before he answered.

"It's you, Abby. The picture on the card is you."

Chapter Eight

"We're not going to get too far with this one." Detective Tim Hayes jerked his thumb toward the yard where the investigative response team worked diligently looking for any incriminating evidence. So far, apparently, they'd found none.

The frozen earth was unforgiving this time of year, and the tape and postcard had yielded no obvious prints. Both had been sent back to the lab for further analysis.

"What about the card itself?" Jack asked, shoving his hands farther into his pockets, trying to ignore the sensation of bitter cold leaching through his skin and into his bones.

Lord, he hated the cold.

Why did people choose to live here?

Hayes blew into his hands, sending a fog of moisture into the night air. "This card has two key differences from the rest." Hayes ticked off the points on his fingers. "Number one, the subject of the photograph is still alive."

Beside Jack, Abby visibly shuddered regardless of the knit cap pulled low over her forehead and ears and the heavy wool coat into which she'd bundled.

Jack should have insisted she wait inside where it was warmer, where she couldn't overhear this conversation.

"Number two," Hayes continued, "This is no modeling shot. Whoever took this probably used that same window to watch and photograph your moves."

"Any idea of when this was taken," Jack asked, shifting his stance so that Abby would know the question was meant for her.

She nodded. "Last night. Right before I found the second card. I'd just been in my kitchen."

Last night.

So much had happened in the past two days. It was a wonder Abby was still on her feet, though based on the circles beneath her eyes and the exhausted tone of her voice, she wouldn't be on her feet for long.

Whoever had taken the photo must have been somewhere in this general area.

Jack glanced from Abby's kitchen window to the house next door where Dwayne Franklin unabashedly watched from a darkened window.

The angle looked right. For all they knew, Franklin had taken the shot, printed off the photograph and taped the postcard to Abby's window.

By now, news of the postcards had begun to spread. No major news stories had broken, but anyone familiar with Abby's blog knew there had been at least two cards.

What was to keep someone out for attention—like Franklin—from trying a little scare tactic of his own?

And if whoever had left the card hadn't been Franklin, chances were pretty damned good Franklin had seen the entire thing. Jack had yet to visit Abby's apartment that he hadn't spotted Franklin waiting and watching.

Regardless of the role Dwayne Franklin had played, whoever left this postcard had been too close to Abby.

Jack had to operate on the belief that the postcard was a legitimate threat from an as-yet-unseen foe.

What if Jack hadn't been here tonight?

Would whoever had left the card have stopped at the window? Or would he have left the postcard as a message once he'd abducted Abby?

What if the card had been left by Boone Shaw? What if all of Jack's ruminations about copycats and attention-seeking neighbors were bull?

He had to proceed as if the threat to Abby had just been kicked up to the next level. From this moment on, Jack stayed with Abby, and she with him. No matter what.

He waited for the police to finish taking statements and questioning neighbors before he made his next move. Gina had arrived to offer moral support and Abby had moved inside. The two women sat huddled together in the living room, nursing steaming mugs of tea. From what Jack had overheard, Robert was on his way over.

Surrounded by her friends, Abby would be safe.

Besides, Jack wasn't going far.

He passed Robert on the sidewalk headed toward Abby's door as Jack headed in the opposite direction. Abby's partner shot Jack a look so cold he felt his blood slow.

"Maybe she was right about you." Uncensored vehemence hung in Robert's voice. "Maybe you started all this to resurrect your case. Maybe you're simply using Abby and our site to fuel your work."

Jack read the look on the other man's face, a mix of anger and protectiveness. Was Robert Walker in love with Abby? Abby insisted the two were nothing more than friends, but perhaps she had no idea of the emotion she apparently inspired in her *friend*.

Jack bit down the annoyance simmering in his gut. He didn't like Robert, although he could say that about a lot of people he'd met over the years. But Jack's dislike for

Robert rose from something deeper, something instinctual, something he hadn't yet put his finger on.

"I have no intention or need to use Abby," Jack said flatly. "If you'll excuse me, I've got work to do."

Yet as Jack walked away, Robert's words took hold deep inside Jack's brain. Of course he was using Abby. He'd set out to do just that. He'd traveled to Delaware to do whatever it took to bring Emma's killer to justice. And he'd intended to destroy Don't Say a Word, if necessary.

Jack might not like Robert Walker, but the man was spot-on about Jack's intentions, much as Jack didn't appreciate the observation.

The curtain at the side window of the house next door swept shut, belying the presence of Dwayne Franklin, lurking at the window. Watching.

Dwayne Franklin studied every move Abby made. A classic stalker, or at least a stalker in the making.

Protectiveness welled inside Jack, and this time he did nothing to bury or deny the feeling. This time he let the emotion infuse him with determination.

He thought of the look of sheer horror on Abby's face when she'd discovered the card.

If Franklin were responsible for putting that fear in her eyes, Jack was sure as hell going to make sure the man never put that same look there again.

He climbed the duplex's front steps, noting the way the concrete had begun to crumble in several spots. For all of the attention Franklin allegedly paid to Abby's property, the same couldn't be said for the neglected shrubbery framing his home's entryway. Overgrown holly branches reached out, clawing at Jack's clothing and partially blocking the handrail.

Jack quickly stepped clear, hitting the front door with a sharp knock.

Footfalls sounded on the other side, and through the frosted glass he spotted a shadowy shape approaching, a shadowy shape consistent with Franklin's paunchy build.

Franklin snapped the door open barely six inches—enough to eyeball Jack, not an inch more.

"I already spoke to the real detectives."

Jack bit back the grin that threatened. If this lowlife thought he could put Jack in his place, he'd better think again.

"You remember my badge, correct?"

Franklin nodded.

"Maybe this time you'd like to see my gun?"

The other man blinked, his gaze narrowing.

"Open the door, Mr. Franklin. I'll take five minutes of your time, then I'll be on my way."

Franklin did as Jack requested, allowing Jack access to a wide, paneled foyer. The apartment door at the end of the hall sat partially open, consistent with the location of the window in which Jack had spotted Abby's neighbor surveying the scene.

"Why don't we step into your apartment?" Jack did his best to force a cordial tone.

"Why don't we skip that step?" Franklin replied.

Much as Jack wanted to get inside Franklin's space, he wasn't about to press the man. Not yet. He'd save intimidation for later. Now wasn't the time.

Besides, if Detective Hayes or one of his team had been inside Franklin's apartment, Jack would be privy to a full description of Franklin's living space.

"I know you've already spoken with the Wilmington detectives, but I wonder if you could answer a few questions for me?"

Franklin visibly stiffened. "I already told them I didn't see a thing."

Jack considered his next move, considered it carefully, deciding to go directly for the information he needed most.

"I saw you at that window—" Jack gestured toward the doorway to the man's apartment "—every single time I glanced at this house tonight. Are you going to tell me you didn't see what happened?"

"I was watching a movie." Franklin gave a dramatic shrug. "So sue me. No one pays me to play neighborhood watch."

"Then who did I see at the window?"

Another shrug. "I haven't the slightest idea."

A sour smell teased the edges of Jack's senses. Urine? Stale clothing? He couldn't place the odor, but he knew the smell originated from Dwayne's apartment. Heaven only knew what lay on the other side of the door.

Jack attempted a step in that direction, but Franklin moved to block him.

"No warrant, no search."

"Warrant? Search?" Jack chuckled. "Who said anything about a warrant or a search? This is a friendly visit to see if you saw the same man Abby saw at her window."

He watched his bluff hit its intended mark. Franklin frowned, then twisted up his features.

"I thought she found some sort of a card stuck to the window? I didn't hear that she saw anyone."

"To the best of my knowledge, the police haven't released specifics, so I'm not at liberty to discuss that."

"But you were inside her apartment when it happened, right?"

So Jack had been right. Dwayne Franklin hadn't missed a trick.

Jack nodded, watching a mix of anger and jealousy play across Franklin's face. "I thought maybe you'd seen the same man. I know how much you'd want to help her."

"I've never done anything but help Abby." Franklin's voice grew shrill, defensive. "I think you're trying to trick me. I'm not an idiot, Detective, and I didn't see a thing."

With that, Franklin turned and raced back to the sanctity of his apartment, slamming the door behind him.

Jack chuckled as he headed back toward the front steps.

If Detective Hayes hadn't told Franklin about the postcard, Franklin had just tipped his hand. He also would have just explained how it was that he hadn't seen anyone at Abby's window.

Dwayne Franklin hadn't seen anyone leave the postcard, because he'd left the postcard himself.

Jack called Hayes's cell before he headed back into Abby's apartment, getting the answers he expected. Franklin had held off the detectives at the doorway, just as he'd done with Jack.

He'd also mentioned the postcard, although none of the responders had released that information.

Much as Jack wanted to point an accusatory finger, he couldn't. Not yet. Anyone watching the house closely enough could have spotted the postcard and recognized it for what it was, and Franklin sure as hell watched Abby's house closely.

The man was a threat to Abby whether she believed Jack or not. Her neighbor might not have anything to do with the case other than carrying out a poorly executed copycat effort aimed at gaining her attention, but he was a menace, just the same.

"You wouldn't be meddling in my case now, would you, Jack?" Hayes's voice pulled Jack's focus free of his myriad thoughts.

"Just being neighborly," Jack lied, glancing over his shoulder just as the curtain at Dwayne Franklin's side window swung shut.

"I DON'T CARE what you think." Robert drained the beer Abby had offered him, his cheeks flushed with color. "The guy doesn't care a thing about your safety. He cares about solving his case. End of story."

Abby's headache had built to a pulsating, pounding intensity that had taken on a life of its own.

As much as she appreciated his show of testosterone, she'd never known Robert to be anything but disagreeable when it came to welcoming new people into his trust. She was in no mood to discuss his current dislike of Jack Grant.

"I think you sound jealous." Gina pursed her lips and nodded. "Matter of fact, I know you sound jealous. Besides, Detective Grant was here with Abby when the card was left. I seriously doubt he tiptoed outside, stuck it to the window and tiptoed back in."

Annoyance flickered in Robert's gaze. As close as they were, he was sometimes irritated by Gina's less-than-tactful way of saying what she thought. "That's not what I'm suggesting."

Gina raised one dark brow in question.

"What I'm saying is that I don't trust him. I never said I thought he hand-delivered the cards."

"Then why don't you trust him?" Abby's voice visibly startled her two friends, as if they'd forgotten she were in the room. "He's here because he thinks the cards might lead him to his sister's killer." She kept her voice low and soft on purpose, hoping her tone might somehow diffuse the growing tension in the room. "I can't fault him for that. Can you?"

Gina pursed her lips again, this time shaking her head. Robert glared at Abby, silent momentarily before he let loose.

"I can't believe how quickly you bought his line of bull." Robert's features tensed. "You believe the justice system set Boone Shaw free?" Robert jerked his thumb toward the outside. "Your detective probably tampered with evidence or screwed something up. You'll see. All this has less to do with catching a killer than it does with Jack Grant easing his guilty conscience."

Abby drew in a slow, steady breath, deciding it was better not to tell Robert she'd find almost as much sympathy for wanting to ease a guilty conscience as she did for wanting to solve the case.

"You need to spend less time dreaming up conspiracy theories, and more time getting some sleep." Gina patted Robert on the shoulder. "I mean, you do lean toward the miserable side, but you're way over the edge tonight."

Robert spun on her. "I suppose you're okay with whoever this madman is putting a postcard of Abby on her window? What happens when her detective isn't here? Who protects her then?"

"Seems to me that's all the more reason you'd like Jack," Abby said. "He promised me he's not going to leave me alone until this nightmare is over and done with."

Gina nodded. "That detective is a man you can trust."

Jack walked through the door before Robert had a chance to respond. Robert chose that moment to grab his coat, brush past the detective, and leave without saying another word.

"Something I said?" Jack scowled at the door as it slammed shut.

Abby forced a smile, when she felt like doing anything but. "He's upset about tonight, that's all."

"Lord, you find an excuse for everyone." Gina reached for her own coat and pushed to her feet.

"Where were you?" Abby asked Jack, choosing to ignore Gina's comment.

"Wanted to ask your neighbor a few questions."

"He had nothing to do with this." Anger and fatigue bristled the hairs at the base of Abby's neck.

Gina pointed at Abby. "Do not try to excuse Dwayne Franklin. That guy is up to no good." She shifted her focus to Jack. "Did she tell you he goes through her mail? It gives me the creeps. I saw him earlier tonight and told him to mind his own business and get a life."

"He's lonely and he looks out for me. He's harmless." But the sudden chill tap dancing down Abby's spine belied her words. "Did he tell you anything, Jack?"

Jack's stare locked on Abby's, making her insides squirm. "Enough for me to distrust him even more than I did before."

Gina crossed to the door with such sharp movements her blunt-cut dark hair swung against her face. As much as Abby loved and appreciated her friend, she'd had just about all of Gina's brassiness she could take for one night. What she needed now was quiet…and sleep.

Gina shrugged into her coat. Her features went serious as she turned to Abby then retraced her steps to give her a hug.

Abby would be lying if she didn't admit her friend's embrace was welcomed and needed.

"Call me," Gina whispered in her ear, as soft-spoken now as she'd been arrogant not a moment earlier. "I can be here in minutes. I'd still feel better if you'd come stay with me, but as long as you won't be alone, I'm okay with you staying here."

"She won't be alone." Jack's deep voice broke the close moment between the two lifelong friends.

"Don't forget to call me," Gina said as she backed toward the door.

"Gina." Abby moved quickly to follow her friend. "I forgot to thank you for the frame." Abby had completely forgotten about the repaired glass amidst the chaos of the night.

Amusement danced in Gina's dark look. "Frame?"

Abby pointed to the picture of the three friends, the once-broken glass now intact. "I broke the glass the other day when Dwayne was here. Did you fix it when you were here earlier?"

Gina pursed her lips, giving her head a slow shake. "It wasn't me. Maybe your little neighbor does more than watch your house while you're not here."

With her parting shot delivered, Gina slipped out the door and into the bitter night, leaving Abby and Jack alone.

Before Abby could thank Jack for everything he'd done, he spoke. "She's right, you know."

"About Dwayne?"

Jack moved two steps closer to where Abby stood, arms wrapped defensively around her waist. "Could be, but I was talking about staying here. You can't."

"And just where I am supposed to go in the middle of the night, Jack?"

"Let me take care of that."

Mind-numbing fatigue washed through her and Abby decided then and there that she didn't have another argument left in her just then, not for Robert, not for Gina and not for Jack.

"I need to sleep. I'll go wherever you want me to go in the morning, but for now, I need to sleep."

Before Jack could so much as say a word, Abby turned and headed for her bedroom. She opened the hall closet as she passed, pulling her overnight bag down from the top shelf.

She'd pack in the morning. She'd listen to Jack then.

But for now, she wanted nothing more than to pretend tonight had never happened, even though she knew the memory of her image on the postcard and the sender's eerie message would most likely haunt her every dream.

Chapter Nine

Abby unpacked her overnight bag, tucking her clothing into the drawers of a hand-painted period piece.

She'd been amazed when she'd woken up and read the bedside clock back at her apartment. Eleven-thirty. She couldn't remember the last time she'd slept so late. Of course, she also couldn't remember the last time she'd pulled an all-nighter or had her life turned so thoroughly on its ear.

She'd awakened to the smell of bacon, eggs and freshly brewed coffee, and as she'd watched Jack work in her kitchen as though he belonged there, something inside her had shifted. Something that she'd long denied. The part of her that wanted to be loved and that wanted to love in return.

But fantasies about a future with Jack Grant would be little more than the work of an overactive imagination. Yes, Abby had seen the undeniable attraction in his eyes when he looked at her. She was fairly sure she wasn't so far out of practice that she'd forgotten how to read the romantic signs. But Jack wasn't here for Abby. Jack was here for his sister, her memory and the memories of the other victims.

He was here to find the truth.

And as Abby watched him carefully prepare her breakfast she knew helping him had become her first priority.

Perhaps by helping Jack find justice for Emma and the others, Abby would find a way to forgive herself for the role she'd played—or hadn't played—in Vicki's death.

"I'd like you to look at the case files, if you think you can handle it."

Jack's words and his accompanying knock at the door to the suite's bedroom jolted her from her memories of a few hours ago.

They'd eaten brunch, packed up enough clothing for Abby to stay away for a few days and then they'd checked Jack out of his hotel.

He'd driven to the Inn at Brandywine Valley, a one-of-a-kind resort that boasted several small suites, free-standing homes once used by workers operating the local gun powder production.

The inn's owners, Sharron and Harold Segroves, had welcomed Jack and Abby with open arms. They'd ushered the pair to their suite loaded down with fresh fruit, pastries and that morning's *Sunday News Journal*.

The suite itself was small, but lovely, appointed with antique furnishings and lush draperies reminiscent of a centuries-old wildflower garden.

"I want you to understand what Boone Shaw is capable of," Jack explained.

Abby slid the drawers of the antique bureau shut. "Do you still believe he's responsible?"

"I believe he's responsible for the New Mexico murders, yes. But I'm not sure he's responsible for the postcards or for Beverly Bricken's murder."

Abby stepped toward Jack, drawn to the unflinching strength reflected in his eyes. "Who then?"

"A student? An admirer? A stranger?" Jack shut his eyes and grimaced, a fleeting glimpse of the toll the investigation had taken on his spirit.

He straightened, locking stares with Abby and forcing a tight smile so quickly Abby wondered if she'd imagined the momentary display of emotion.

She moved so close she could smell the fresh scent of the soap he'd used in her shower that morning. She reached toward his face, but stopped herself short of touching his clean-shaven cheek.

His features remained impassive, unreadable. "You can't trust anyone, Abby. Not anymore."

"What about you, Jack?"

The tension between them grew palpable, but Jack didn't so much as blink. He also didn't answer her question, turning toward the living area and gesturing for her to join him at the small dining table.

"Your investigator hasn't found Shaw?"

A muscle in Jack's jaw tensed then released, then tensed again. "I plan to call him in a bit, but at last check, Boone Shaw's financial activity showed no movement, no deposits, no withdrawals, no charges."

"So he could be anywhere?"

"Or we could be chasing a ghost."

The word sent a shudder through Abby as she eyed the fat case folder Jack pulled from his briefcase.

"You don't think the card last night is the same guy, do you?" she asked.

Jack's gaze locked with hers, holding her captive with the intensity of his stare. "I think last night might very well have been the work of a copycat, but I won't risk your safety either way."

"You're saying I'm not in danger if it was a copycat?"

"You're safer if the copycat is only out for attention. I can't risk that he's not out to copy the original crimes. I also can't risk that my gut instinct is off for some reason and last night's card is legit."

Jack spoke surely and strongly, a man confident in thought and action, a man unfazed by the events of the past two days.

"How often has your gut instinct been wrong?"

"Never." He dropped his focus back to the folder, removing the contents and studying each piece of paper, each photo as if he might see something he'd never seen there before.

"Is that the original file?" Abby asked. "Or a copy?"

"Copy."

"They let you do that?"

"*They* don't have to know."

She stepped toward him, trying not to gawk at the crime scene photos he'd pulled from the folder. As she neared, Jack slid the photos beneath a sheet of bullet point notes, hand-written, perhaps something he'd compiled over the years.

"Are you protecting them? Or me?"

"Both." He looked up at her and frowned. "Do you always ask so many questions?"

Abby ignored his question, settling into an empty chair at the table. She sat without saying another word, watching him move through the notes, through the transcripts of what she imagined to be testimony, through the photos of the missing and the dead.

Jack's hand stilled when he came across the crime scene marked with a large number two. His sister Emma. Even in death, she'd been a breathtaking young woman, taken too soon from a life too short.

"You and me, we're not so different after all, are we?" Abby asked.

Jack humored her with a reply. "How so?"

"We're haunted by what we might have done differently."

Something deep inside Jack's penetrating gaze shifted, and for a moment Abby glimpsed the raw grief he still held there. Then just as quickly, the look was gone, and Jack dropped his focus back to the file contents.

"I let go of the guilt a long time ago."

"Did you?"

He said nothing, instead tucking the notes and printouts and photos back into the folder.

"I see it in your eyes, Jack," Abby continued. She knew she was pushing her luck, pushing the man, but she couldn't help herself.

Something about Jack Grant made her want to help him, made her want to pull him into her arms and tell him he wasn't to blame for his sister's death.

A madman was to blame. A madman Jack had chased for eleven years, never once accepting the defeat he'd faced years ago as anything but temporary.

He closed the folder, returned it to his briefcase, then pushed to his feet. "This was a bad idea."

Abby stood, facing him head-on. "None of this is your fault."

"You," his voice dropped low, so distant it chilled Abby to the core, "don't know a thing about me or my faults. Let's keep it that way."

He turned to walk away, but Abby followed, reaching for his arm. "Let me get this straight. You can sit in my house lecturing me on letting go of my guilt, telling me I couldn't have done a thing to save Vicki, but I'm not allowed to say so much as boo to you about your sister's death?"

He pulled his arm free of her touch, leaving her fingers cold. "Sounds about right."

JACK SHUT THE bedroom door behind him and swore beneath his breath.

Damn Abby Conroy.

None of this is your fault.

For someone he'd expected to be a pushover, she'd proven to be anything but, and he admired her for the annoying trait. How could he not? But he wasn't about to sit across the table from her, holding hands and sharing psychobabble.

If she thought he was a man who wanted to get in touch with his feelings, she'd best think again.

The only thing Jack wanted to get in touch with was whoever had sent the cards, and he was growing more and more certain he was chasing more than one man.

He pulled out his cell and dialed Max in Montana.

Jack and Max had gone through the Academy together, and after a few years on the force, Max had decided the life of a private investigator suited him better than that of a police officer.

Max had apparently made a smart choice.

Jack had yet to hear of a case Max hadn't been able to unravel.

Jack could only hope this case wouldn't be the one to break Max's streak.

The private investigator answered on the first ring. "I was waiting for your call."

"You have something for me?"

Max blew out a whistle. "Matter of fact, I've got a whole lot of nothing for you."

"So why do you sound excited?"

"Because that nothing comes at the end of a trip east that ended not far from where you are now."

"Shaw's here?" Jack's pulse quickened. "You've got a location for me?"

If Max had found Boone Shaw, Jack's investigation had just taken a huge leap forward.

"Not a one," Max answered.

Jack let loose a string of expletives. "Are you playing with me, Max? Because things are escalating here and I don't have time for games."

"Apparently Shaw didn't have time for games, either. Told his wife he had to take care of business before it was too late."

Too late? "For what?"

"Dying." Silence beat across the line before Max explained. "Lung cancer. Stage four. He's probably only got weeks left to live."

"Sonofa—"

Someone that ill didn't strike Jack as a likely candidate for sending the cards or posing a threat to Abby, unless the man was trying to go out with a bang.

"Did the wife say what business it was Boone had to take care of?"

"She did." Another pause.

"And?" Impatience flared inside Jack, but he knew better than to push Max. The investigator enjoyed a dramatic delivery, always had.

"She said he wanted to clear his name before he died. Wanted to bring the real killer to justice once and for all."

"Well, what do you know…" Jack's voice trailed off on the last word. If Boone Shaw and his wife were telling the truth, Shaw and Jack had wanted the same thing all these years.

Jack wasn't buying a word.

"Does she know where he is?" he asked.

"No idea. Cell phone appears to be dead or disabled. He hasn't called her in over ten days, and he hasn't returned a single voice mail."

"Damn."

"But she knows where he was."

Another pause. Jack clenched his fist, wishing he had a drink right about now, something he hadn't thought in a long time.

"Where, Max?"

"Elkton, Maryland. Said he'd found his man and was set to make contact the next day."

Elkton, Maryland. Less than forty minutes to the south of Wilmington. Too close to be coincidence.

"Nothing since?"

"Nothing."

"What about hotel possibilities?"

"Nothing on credit, but I'm working through the list."

"How many?"

"Not bad. Less than twenty."

Jack let out a long whistle. "That's a nice break. You'll let me know if you find anything?"

"The second I find it."

"Thanks, Max."

"I've got a package waiting for you, Jack."

"On a Sunday?"

Max laughed. "Hey, when you're good, you're good. I happen to be very good."

"So you keep telling me." Jack smiled, glad for the light moment in what had quickly become a very heavy day.

Jack fumbled in the nightstand drawer for pen and paper as Max rattled off the address and phone number for a local business center and shipping outlet.

Jack repeated the information, double-checking accuracy, then thanked Max for calling. He flipped to the map in the front of the phonebook, located the general vicinity of the shipping outlet address and noted the direction he'd need to take from the inn to hit the correct shopping center.

He found Abby standing in the suite's kitchen, staring out the small window over the sink.

"Deep thoughts?"

She spoke without turning to look at him, frustration evident in her tone and stance. "You're a real jerk, Grant."

"I've been called worse."

When she did turn to face him, one corner of her mouth lifted into a crooked grin. "Good."

The woman was like no one—male or female—Jack had met before. Stubborn, beautiful and sharp as a tack. Abby Conroy was a force to be reckoned with, a force he hadn't anticipated or expected, and a force that was slowly eating away at his resolve to do nothing more than use her for information then turn and walk away.

Jack did something then that he rarely did. He apologized. "Sorry about before."

She closed the space between them, standing so near he could feel the heat of her body. "You asked me whether I started the site to assuage my guilt or to help others," she said, her eyes never leaving his, heating his insides with the depth of her scrutiny.

"I asked you about Emma because I genuinely wanted the answer. I wanted to know if I could help you somehow. I've been standing here ever since wondering why in the hell I care. Any ideas?"

Jack shook his head, but even as he did so, he lowered his mouth to hers, tasting tentatively at first before he took her mouth with his, covering her lips, easing them apart with his tongue to kiss her so deeply, passionately, that he thought some unseen force had taken over his every instinct.

Jack pulled her into his arms, reveling in the feel of her fingertips as they found the nape of his neck. The lush curves of her breasts pressed into his chest and he hardened instantly, unable to control his body's reaction to holding her, tasting her, wanting her.

Abby pulled away, bright color staining her cheeks. "And I had you pegged as emotionally distant."

Jack scrubbed a hand across his face, remorse flooding his every nerve and muscle, even as his body screamed for a deeper joining with Abby. "Mistake. Big mistake."

He brushed past her, headed for the door.

"Jack?"

He ignored her, not willing to risk what he might do next if he stayed in the suite. "I'll be back. Do not leave this room."

But as he drove away from the inn, Jack realized it wasn't kissing Abby he regretted, it was walking away. And that thought scared Jack almost as much as the realization that more than forty-eight hours into his investigation, he was no closer to the truth than he'd been the moment he'd taken Herb Simmons's call.

Only now, one critical element had shifted.

Abby Conroy had become far more than a means to an end. She'd become a target.

Jack needed to regain his control, his focus. He needed to be at the top of his game to keep her safe, and suddenly, keeping her safe had become priority number one.

Caving to a physical hunger was a risk he couldn't take, a distraction he couldn't afford.

No matter how much he wanted to.

Chapter Ten

Abby seethed with anger and frustration. She didn't need Jack Grant, his so-called protection or his mind-numbing kiss.

She winced, remembering the way she'd eagerly pressed her body to his, the way she'd raked her fingers up through his hair, the way she'd come alive at the contact of their bodies—skin to skin, lip to lip, heat to heat.

She shook her head, muttering to herself as she headed back toward her bedroom.

She couldn't stay here. She couldn't sleep under the same roof as the man. He couldn't be trusted. For all she knew, he'd jump her in the middle of the night.

She could only hope.

Abby groaned, unable to believe her mind had become consumed by thoughts of being with Jack instead of thoughts of the threatening postcard bearing her photograph.

A solid dose of reality washed through her, grounding her, dimming the memory of being in Jack's arms, albeit briefly.

Thank God she'd insisted on bringing her car, the car she planned to drive straight back to her apartment. She'd call Gina and ask her to come over. That way, Abby wouldn't be alone and Jack couldn't accuse her of being foolish.

Conflicting thoughts and urges battled for space inside her brain and she shook her head. She'd figure it all out once she got home…to her apartment, her space, her things.

She had a right to be there. A right to stake her claim and refuse to be driven out of her own apartment.

Abby left her overnight bag and clothing behind. Right now she needed out of this suite and away from all thoughts of Jack Grant.

She slammed the door to the suite shut behind her, held her head high and headed for her car. The crisp winter air cleared her senses instantly, infusing her with a renewed alertness and determination.

She needed time to regroup emotionally and physically, then she'd be ready to face Jack and the case again.

For now, she planned to leave all thoughts of postcards, killers and frustratingly stubborn detectives behind. And as the image of Jack's face and the memory of his kiss took position first and foremost in her mind, she groaned, realizing that no matter what she told herself, Jack Grant wasn't going anywhere anytime soon.

She was stuck with the man and his case, whether she liked it or not.

THE EXPRESS PACKAGE sat waiting for Jack behind the counter at the nearby Package Plus, just as Max had promised. Not wanting to open the envelope in front of an audience, he headed to the bagel shop next door, ordering a tall black coffee before he settled at a corner table.

Inside the envelope, Max had tucked proof of the claims he'd made over the phone. The transcript of his recorded conversation with Shaw's wife. A copy of the tape-recorded conversation, should Jack want additional backup.

He skimmed the transcript, his gaze settling on random words and phrases. Terminal. Stage four. Death sentence. No contact for the past ten days.

Apparently Shaw had telephoned his wife each evening as he traveled across the country, starting back in his former New Mexico haunts then driving east. The last phone call had been received ten days ago, transmitted through a cell tower in Elkton.

Had Shaw been headed to Wilmington? Had he found the person he sought? And if so, why had he failed to check in with his wife from that point on?

Apparently, the wife had been unable to get anything but voice mail on Shaw's cell phone ever since, leading Jack to believe Shaw had met with either bad luck or foul play. Jack's gut would put money on the latter.

Chances were Boone Shaw had found exactly the person he'd been after, and that person had not been happy about the contact.

Jack flipped through the rest of the documentation. Medical records. Doctor's summaries. The disability paperwork completed once his condition had been deemed terminal.

The logo at the top of a piece of letterhead from Shaw's former studio snagged Jack's attention, tugging at his memory. He skimmed the sheet of paper and the handwritten list. Clients.

Jack recognized the names from his days on the case. Five names in particular—the victims—hit him like a knife to the heart.

What was Shaw after? And why would a gravely ill man leave his home and wife to travel cross-country if he already faced the killer each day in the mirror?

Short answer. He wouldn't.

What if the investigators and prosecutors had zeroed in on the wrong suspect all along? Yet all of the evidence had pointed to Shaw. If Shaw had any idea at all of the real killer's identity, why wouldn't he have provided that information eleven years earlier?

Had he been protecting someone?

Jack flipped open his cell and redialed Max's number. He spoke as soon as the line connected. "Did you find records on children or siblings for Shaw?"

"Nothing. He and his wife never had kids and Shaw was an only child. He came from a small family and he's the last remaining survivor, according to my search."

Another dead end.

Jack pressed a fist to the table, thanked Max for the information and the package, then stared at the evidence.

Don't let him get away again. Herb Simmons's words played in Jack's brain like a broken record.

The original investigation had settled on Shaw for good reason. The man had had the means and the opportunity. The investigation had assigned the motive—sexual predator.

But if the investigation had been focused on the wrong man all along, the trail of the real killer would be colder than cold by now.

Eleven years virtually eliminated the chance a second suspect would be found and convicted…not unless Shaw led Jack to the guilty party.

Jack took another long drink of his coffee and shook the envelope, wanting to be sure he hadn't missed anything.

A black-and-white photo fluttered to the floor, igniting memories of unwanted images from the case file. The victims in life. The victims in death.

Yet the face that greeted Jack when he plucked the

dropped photo from the floor didn't belong to a victim. It belonged to Boone Shaw.

The man was but a shadow of his former self. Gaunt, older and wasted, Shaw's physical appearance left no room for doubt about the man's health.

Jack replayed Max's words in his mind.

He wanted to clear his name before he died.

Based on Shaw's photo, death wasn't too far off. Maybe Shaw hadn't met with foul play at all. Maybe he'd fallen out of contact with his wife because he'd met with fate. Perhaps his time had simply run out.

The ramifications of the evidence spread across the coffee shop table hit Jack like a dead weight between the eyes. Had he been focused on the wrong man from day one?

Maybe Boone Shaw hadn't gotten away with murder. Maybe he'd gotten away with his life after being falsely accused. And now that death held the man in a stare-down contest, Shaw had decided he didn't want to die without clearing his name.

Or was it that Shaw didn't want to die without tying up any loose ends?

What if Shaw hadn't been tracking the killer? What if he'd been tracking the one person with the power to condemn him once and for all?

Jack shook his head. His investigative brain was working overtime, and he wasn't being logical.

A man as ill as Shaw would not travel cross-country to open old wounds. He might, however, do so in order to leave his name and legacy clear, a goodbye gift to his wife, so to speak.

As loath as Jack was to admit it, the simplest theory made the most sense.

Boone Shaw hadn't committed the murderous Christmas killing spree. He hadn't raped and killed five young women. He hadn't killed Emma.

Jack had been after the wrong man for eleven years.

His sense of reality tipped sideways momentarily, then Jack righted himself, regaining control of his thoughts and focus.

His mission hadn't changed: to find the killer by working backward from the postcards.

The only thing that had changed was the target—or rather his opinion of the target.

Jack still needed Shaw. He needed to know exactly who the man was after and why.

Jack gathered the documentation and the photograph, tucking them back into the folder. Then he drained his coffee, pushed out of his chair and headed for the door.

Shaw had been coming this way when he went silent. The time had come to circle the wagons. After all, Jack had zero idea from which direction an attack might come, but he felt it coming.

He had to consider every possibility, and he had to prepare for any feasible development.

A misstep now might cost Abby her safety…or her life, and that was a misstep Jack had no intention of taking.

ABBY REALIZED AS soon as she set foot inside her apartment that she'd made a mistake.

Jack had been correct. She had no business being here. The sofa was still askew from where Jack had slept the night before. Her remaining furniture had been rearranged to accommodate the influx of investigative personnel who had responded to last night's call.

This wasn't her apartment any longer.

This was a crime scene.

She pivoted on her heel, intending to beat a fast path back to the inn with the hope of reaching the suite before Jack returned. With any luck at all, he'd never be the wiser about her excursion, and she'd be spared another lecture about her personal security shortcomings.

Dwayne Franklin stood in the doorway, his slightly overweight frame taking up every available inch of space.

"Dwayne." Abby's voice jumped as sharply as her heart. She hadn't heard so much as a footfall at the threshold behind her.

"I needed to see you." Dwayne's eyes appeared unfocused as he moved toward her.

Abby stood her ground, not wanting to back any farther into her apartment. There was only one exit door, and right now Dwayne Franklin loomed between Abby and her goal.

"Did you see what happened last night, Dwayne?"

He shook his head, taking another step toward her. He stood close enough now to touch her and did so, caressing a lock of her hair between his thumb and forefinger.

Adrenaline pumped to life in Abby's veins, momentarily leaving her unsteady.

"You're making me uncomfortable, Dwayne."

He'd never touched her this way before, never stood this close, and if she wasn't mistaken she could smell alcohol on his breath.

"Have you been drinking?"

The moment she uttered the question, Dwayne spun away from her, slamming his fist against the wall. "I've been cooking. For you. For us."

His sudden, violent outburst left Abby reeling. She had to get out of her apartment and away from Dwayne as quickly as possible.

Something had shifted inside the man. His tone of voice

and the look in his eyes bordered on unstable, flooding Abby with trepidation and dread.

"You're scaring me, Dwayne. I need you to leave."

What if Jack had been right? What if Dwayne had left the postcard? What if he were somehow involved in all of the postcards as a way to get Abby's attention?

"I would never hurt you, Abby. You're my friend."

"I know you're my friend, Dwayne." She struggled to keep her voice calm, soothing, wanting only to reassure Dwayne and get him the hell out of her apartment. "I'm your friend, too."

Dwayne's features darkened, like a storm brewing just beneath the surface of his tentative control. "You're a liar."

Abby took a backward step, as if the force of Dwayne's words had physically pushed her.

"You forgot about our dinner tonight."

Dinner.

Dwayne was right. Abby had completely forgotten. Dwayne had been planning tonight for weeks. He'd wanted to make her dinner, and she'd agreed, thinking the gesture harmless.

How wrong she'd been.

"I'll have to reschedule, Dwayne. I'm sorry."

His voice dropped low and flat, detached. "Why? Because you're going to be with that cop?"

"Yes." Abby nodded, formulating her story even as she spoke it. "Detective Grant is on his way here, now. We have to work tonight. I'm sorry."

Dwayne's stern facade began to crumble and he turned toward the door. "You're not sorry at all. You're just like all the rest."

Before Abby could say another word, Dwayne was gone. The irrational part of her wanted to go after him, wanted to remind him that she'd been his friend when everyone else had steered clear. But the rational part of her won the battle.

   She gathered up her purse and keys and raced for her car, doing her best to ignore the window next door, yet unable to miss the swish of the curtains and the bulky figure watching her as she ran away.

Chapter Eleven

Jack was so angry with Abby he couldn't see straight.

Which part of *do not leave this room* had the woman failed to understand?

Abby recounted the incident with Franklin, repeating their conversation word for word, describing Franklin's actions and demeanor. Jack's gut tightened.

He said nothing for several long moments after she stopped talking, wanting to choose his words carefully. Tact was not the usual response for Jack, but as much as he hated to admit it, he cared about what he said to Abby and how he said it. In addition, the fact Franklin had given Abby the scare of her life was evident in the bright fear still shimmering in her eyes.

"You have to promise me you'll be more careful."

She opened her mouth to say something, but Jack held up a hand to stop her.

"First things first. I want to apologize for what happened between us earlier. I was out of line and I wasn't thinking. It won't happen again."

Jack reached for the express envelope he'd received from Max and pulled Shaw's photo from inside. "This is what I received from my private investigator today. A recent photo of Boone Shaw."

He waited while Abby studied the black-and-white photograph, her eyes going wide.

"I thought you said he was big and brawny?"

"He was. He's dying. And his wife hasn't heard from him in over ten days."

"You don't think he sent the cards?" Abby handed him back the photo and blew out a frustrated breath. "What's going on, Jack?"

"I wish I knew." He filled her in on the intel Max had provided and Shaw's last known location, Elkton.

"We should go." Abby hugged herself, pacing a tight pattern in the living room. Back and forth. Back and forth. "Maybe he's sick somewhere. In the hospital. Still in his room."

"Or dead."

Jack's harsh statement stopped Abby in her tracks and she turned to him, her expression one of surprise.

"We have to be realistic."

"Dead as in sick and died?" she asked. "Or dead as in he found whoever he was looking for and they weren't happy to see him?"

"Don't know." He saw his own frustration mirrored in Abby's expression. "For all we know, Shaw's visit was the trigger that inspired the postcards."

Abby sat at the dining table and lowered her face to her hands. Jack longed to reach out to her, to pull her into his arms, to tell her everything would be all right, but truth was, he couldn't make that promise when he didn't know what was going on. Plus, he didn't trust himself to touch her.

Not now.

"Abby."

She raised her gaze to his, confusion palpable in her pale eyes.

"We don't know what or who we're up against," he

continued. "We've got a lot of theories, but no proof. I need you to trust me."

"I do trust you—"

"Let me finish."

His chest squeezed as he spoke, and Jack realized he couldn't deny how much Abby had come to mean to him, no matter how he tried.

"Maybe Franklin's actions have something to do with this case, or maybe they don't. Maybe the guy is simply obsessed with you. Not a great option, but a step above having a serial killer on your trail.

"But in order for me to keep you safe, I need to know you're where you tell me you're going to be. I need to know you're safe, because if anything happened to you…"

Jack hesitated, not ready to tell Abby Conroy just how far she'd gotten under his skin. "That's it. I need to know where you are at all times."

Shock edged the frustration and confusion tangling for position in Abby's face. The unspoken part of Jack's words hadn't been lost on her, even in her current state of distress.

She moved toward him, taking his hands in hers.

The contact sent a jolt of heat through Jack's system, but he made no move to shift away—part refusal to show her proximity had any effect on him and part desire to be as close to her as possible.

ABBY FOUND HERSELF blown away by Jack's admission, even though he'd caught himself before he'd fully let down his guard.

Her encounter with Dwayne had set the detective on edge. She could see it in his eyes, hear it in his voice, sense it in the tension radiating from his touch.

"I'm sorry." She meant the words as she said them, fully and completely.

She'd screwed up and she knew it. She'd also been damned lucky Dwayne had backed down.

"I'd like to see the case files again, please."

Jack pulled his fingers free from her touch, reaching for his briefcase. "Some of this is fairly graphic."

"I'm a big girl, Jack. I know you want to protect me, but I need you to let me in a bit more. Let me help."

And so he did, pulling the folder from his briefcase and handing it to her, setting the carefully collected reports, notes and photos in her hands, then turning away, trusting her with his work.

He gave her space as she looked through the pages. He remained silent as she studied the photos, processed the available information, the horror of the killings, the loss of bright lives so young.

When she'd finished her review, she turned her focus on Jack, watching him as he watched her, reading the unspoken heartache in his eyes, measuring the weight he carried on his shoulders.

"It wasn't your fault," she said softly.

He narrowed his eyes, frowning. "Big brothers keep little sisters safe. Especially when the big brother is a law enforcement officer. I failed her, Abby, just like I failed each of those families by focusing on the wrong man."

"You didn't act alone. The entire team focused on the wrong man. Obviously the evidence pointed to Boone Shaw. Either you're wrong about his innocence or someone set him up."

"If Max can locate the hotel where he stayed, we'll have a place to start digging."

"What about our local victim?" Abby studied a close up of the eye branded into one of the victim's thighs. "Was she branded like this?"

"Bricken?" Jack nodded. "Similar method apparently, but a completely different mark."

"Like what?"

"A pair of lips."

Abby tipped her head from side to side. "I don't think a pair of lips is that far off from an eye, do you?"

Seeing. Talking. Ignoring.

She replayed Dwayne Franklin's statement in her mind. *You're just like all the rest.*

"Maybe the killer felt ignored. He used the images of an eye and a pair of lips to make his victims pay attention, to make them talk to him."

Jack studied her, visibly impressed. "I hadn't thought about it that way, but a killer's signature rarely changes."

"But the Bricken murder was six years after the others. Wouldn't it make sense that the killer might have changed in that time?"

"Anything's possible."

"Is that why you'd never heard of this case? He branded her with lips instead of an eye?"

Jack nodded. "I'd entered our cases to have the system send up a flag if a similar case hit. Meantime, the local case was coded as a cutting or engraving."

"Not a branding?"

He shook his head. "The database never picked up the similarity."

Genuine frustration pulled at Abby's gut. "Sounds like a lot of room for error."

"You have no idea."

"Do you think Bricken's murder is unrelated? Or a copycat?"

"Could be either." Faint lines bracketed Jack's dark eyes. He'd barely slept since he arrived on the east coast and the stress and exhaustion had begun to take a visible toll. "Or maybe it is my guy somehow."

She needed to get this man a good solid meal and then make sure he rested. But first, she had to be honest about her opinion of the cases.

"I think it's the same guy, Jack. Something about the way she was posed for the modeling shot." Abby pictured the postcards of the two victims and then Bricken's. "Melinda, Emma and Bricken's poses are identical."

"You think so?" He moved to the table, then sat across from her.

She nodded. "A photographer composes his shot just like an artist composes her canvas. The first three pictures were taken by the same person. I'm sure of it."

"And how do we explain that if our theory about Devine planting the postcard holds true?" A light shone in his eyes as they spoke, and Abby realized he was enjoying their give and take, enjoying working through the logic of the case together.

"Maybe he had the photo in his possession ever since he worked the story. Or maybe he didn't plant the postcard at all."

Jack stretched his arms up over his head and let out a groan. "We need to pin Devine down on the source of the photo and locate the hotel used by Boone Shaw."

Abby blinked, surprised and pleased that Jack was treating her as an equal partner. "First things first."

His eyebrows lifted in question.

"Food."

JACK LEANED BACK against his chair, thinking Abby had read his mind. He was starving and he was exhausted, not that he'd admit the latter. Detectives did not admit fatigue. They wore it as a badge of honor.

He couldn't help but notice that Abby had avoided all talk of the most recent postcard. "You haven't mentioned your photo."

"We both know I didn't pose for it." The smile she forced didn't reach her eyes. Jack knew she was trying to hide the fact the threatening message had left her unnerved.

But she was right about one thing. The fourth card was different, more different than just the style of photograph.

"Hayes called," he said matter-of-factly. "The fourth photograph was printed on completely different paper from the first three shots."

The local detective had called Jack as he drove back from Package Plus. The lab had completed its initial analysis of the photo paper used in each card.

"The lab says the photo paper used in your card is completely different from the others—a specialty stock only sold locally and not meant for printing high-resolution photography."

Confusion flashed in Abby's eyes. "A professional wouldn't make that mistake."

"Exactly."

"And the other three?" she asked.

Jack moved toward the door. "Same manufacturer, though it's the most common on the market."

"So not necessarily from the same source?"

"Correct."

"Has anyone checked out the specialty paper?"

Jack nodded, wishing he had better news. "Hayes visited the shop himself. No one there recognized either Shaw or Devine from their photos. He didn't have a photo of Franklin."

Abby frowned. She'd never seen a photo of Dwayne, come to think of it, but that didn't mean she couldn't find a way to get one.

"If Dwayne left that card for me, would he be charged with a crime?"

Frustration flashed across Jack's face. "Strong possibility, but that would depend on you."

"What are my choices?"

"Loitering, stalking, harassment." Jack shrugged.

Before today Abby wouldn't have thought her neighbor capable of any crime, but now...now she wasn't so sure. Based on the violent outburst she'd witnessed, he might very well be a danger to himself, if not others.

"What do you know about his background?" Jack asked.

"I've asked him, but he always changes the subject." She realized how foolish the statement sounded as soon as she spoke.

"I'll have Max run a check." He pulled open the door and gestured for Abby to join him. "In the meantime, what do you say you and I enjoy the inn's restaurant and give ourselves some time off?"

A bright smile lit Abby's face as she moved to his side, and Jack realized he wouldn't mind seeing her smile every day from here on out. Part of him couldn't blame Dwayne Franklin for fixating on the woman. She was friendly, intelligent and breathtaking.

Then Franklin's cold, calculating eyes flashed through Jack's mind and a fresh wave of anger crested inside him. "Maybe Franklin thought he could scare you then step in and play the savior."

Abby's brows disappeared beneath her fringe of bangs. "Seems to me that role's already been spoken for."

Her words took Jack by surprise. Did Abby think that's what he'd done? Put himself in a position to play savior?

Her grin widened. "You don't have to look so stunned, Detective, I know you're only doing your job."

But as they headed across the grounds of the inn toward the main building, Jack couldn't seem to wrench his thoughts from her words.

Was he only doing his job?

Or had his concern for Abby's safety become something much more? He was physically attracted to her. Of that, there was no doubt. Jack was fairly certain the feeling was mutual.

He'd apologized for kissing her and had given Abby his word it wouldn't happen again. Jack was determined to keep that promise.

When this investigation concluded, Jack would return to Arizona, leaving Abby and Delaware far behind.

Yet the more time he spent with the woman, the more difficult he found the truth to deny.

His feelings for Abby had become personal. Very personal. And a big part of Jack's focus now would be keeping those feelings from interfering with what had rapidly become a very complicated investigation.

HE STOOD INSIDE Abby Conroy's home, moving slowly through her things—her furniture, her books, her belongings. He sensed her, felt her, smelled the clean scent of her cosmetics, lingering still as if she'd just stepped out of the shower.

But she wasn't here.

The detective had moved her to safer ground.

Smart, yet not impossible to overcome. After all, sooner or later, the woman would return to work. He'd find her there, wait until she was alone, then make his move.

Abby Conroy didn't strike him as a woman who would tolerate the limits the good detective had placed on her for long.

Anyone who read her blog or had read the *People*

profile would understand that her work at Don't Say a Word defined her.

She wouldn't let anything keep her away from the blog, the postcards, the confessors.

Abby Conroy was far too stubborn to let a menacing message on a postcard scare her off for good. He was counting on it.

Sure, the woman could write her blogs from afar, but she couldn't check her mail, touch the handmade cards, feel part of her readers' lives.

And so, he'd wait, and he'd plan his moves accordingly, allowing for the possible choices Abby Conroy might make.

She'd proven to be no better than the others had been. She hadn't made time for him, listened to him, talked to him.

She'd ignored him.

He hated to be ignored.

The man's blood boiled and he brought a fist down on a table. Hard.

A framed photograph toppled over, and he righted the frame, deciding to borrow the keepsake from the shelf.

So much for not leaving any trace of his visit.

With any luck at all, Abby Conroy wouldn't notice the picture missing. Hell, she didn't notice anything except her precious blog site as it was.

He stared down into the objects of the photo—Abby and two other young women. Friends for life, supposedly.

And then it hit him, a moment of clarity so strong and pure it nearly stole his breath away.

He knew exactly how to reach Abby Conroy, exactly how to pull her out of hiding and into his plan.

He'd go after those she held most dear.

And he knew exactly where to start.

Chapter Twelve

Abby's cell phone rang a little after six-thirty the next morning.

"Where in the hell are you?" Robert's voice dripped with anger.

"Did we have plans?"

"No, but I'm standing in the freezing cold at your front door with today's *News Journal* and you're apparently nowhere to be found. At least, that's what your nosy neighbor told me."

"Dwayne?"

"I'm telling you the guy's interest in you isn't natural." The fact Robert had the decency to drop his voice low when he voiced his opinion of Dwayne wasn't lost on Abby.

"That's funny, Robert. Jack says the same thing about you."

"Jack?" The anger returned, a sharp edge breaking through Robert's control. "We're on a first-name basis now?"

Based on the anger and jealousy in her partner's voice, Abby realized Jack might have been correct in his assessment of Robert. Did he have feelings for Abby? Feelings she'd never read properly?

"Where are you?" he repeated, this time in a growl.

"I can't tell you."

"You can't *tell* me? I'm not some masked murderer here, Abby."

This was Robert, for crying out loud, and she was being overly secretive. "The Inn at Brandywine Valley, just until Jack and the police figure out what's going on."

Silence beat across the line. When Robert spoke again, the control had returned to his tone, as if he'd taken the time to compose himself.

"I don't suppose you and your detective have seen today's paper yet?"

"Why?"

"You might want to pick up a copy. I think it's safe to say Sam Devine decided to take your little story and run with it."

Five minutes later, Abby had pulled on a thermal shirt, down vest and jeans and had tugged her knit cap over her head. There were no signs of life from Jack's room as she headed through the suite, then jogged over to the main building.

"Morning, Abby," Sharron Segroves called out.

"Morning," Abby answered, gathering up two cups of coffee and two bagels in her effort to look calm, cool and collected when all she really wanted to do was grab a copy of the paper and race back to the suite.

Harold Segroves walked briskly past, carrying a steaming tray of bacon. "Morning, Abby. Tucked a paper under the desk for you. Wanted to make sure you got a copy."

"Morning." Abby frowned. "And thanks, I think."

Harold slowed and turned, talking to Abby while walking backward. "Jack confided in us when you all first checked in. He asked us to keep an eye out for anything strange. Knew you'd want to see that article first thing."

Abby thanked the inn's owner again, then braced herself as she ducked her head behind the reception desk. She wasn't sure what she expected, but certainly not the monstrous front page headline that waited on the desk's center shelf.

Home for the Holidays. Has the Christmas Confessor Moved East?

Abby snapped the paper from the shelf, zeroing in on the byline. Sam Devine.

So much for trying to keep the media from turning recent events into a circus.

"Bastard."

"My thoughts exactly." The rich timbre of Jack's voice took the edge off of Abby's shock, but she stumbled trying to juggle the paper, the coffee and the bagels as she backed out of the small space.

Jack smiled warmly as he reached for her hands, then gripped her arm, helping her straighten away from the desk.

They'd turned the corner during the dinner they'd shared with the Segroves the night before. Instead of mulling possible suspects and motives, they'd conversed like adults out for a relaxing meal. And they'd enjoyed themselves.

Jack's smile was testament to the fact the comfort level between them had increased ten-fold at some point during the evening.

They'd both gone to their bedrooms after the meal, but Abby had tossed and turned most of the night, wondering whether the attraction she felt for Jack was due to their forced proximity, or whether it could be something more. Something real.

"I thought you were still asleep," Abby said.

Jack shook his head. "Met Tim Hayes for an early

breakfast. I wanted to update him on our end of the investigation."

"Anything new from him?" Abby asked, hope welling inside her.

"Not a thing. So we talked about this." He tapped the front of the paper.

"I just heard." Abby flipped open the paper, grimacing at the black-and-white images plastered across the page. Melinda Simmons. Emma. Beverly Bricken. "Sorry, Jack."

He waved off her comment. "Been there, done that. If Devine's lucky he'll get one follow-up assignment to this insubstantial mess. There's nothing here except the ruminations of a reporter who missed his boat years ago."

He pointed to an inset shot. "One tiny point of note."

Abby followed his gesture, her breath catching at the picture, a shot of the investigative team's response to the card taped to her window.

"So he was there that night?" she asked, unable to remember seeing anyone but officers and friends.

"Apparently so, though who knows how far away." Jack picked up the coffees and bagels and tipped his head toward the door. Abby followed. "Or, he hired a freelancer. Those guys are masters at pulling off a shot like that unnoticed."

"How about a shot through someone's kitchen window?" Abby took one of the coffees from Jack and swallowed big. "Needs whiskey."

"Now, now." Jack pushed the door open with his hip and made room for Abby to pass. "Let's not let a fame-hungry reporter drive us to drink. Let's stick to the plan."

"Which is?"

"You go to work as usual, with one exception."

Abby grinned. "I know this one. I have my own security detail."

"At your service, ma'am." Jack laughed, the sound genuine and spontaneous, warming Abby from the inside out. "Now then, let's get this show on the road."

"What about Devine?"

"Don't worry about him," Jack answered, a muscle in his jaw twitching. "Let's worry about how the *Confessor* plans to respond to Devine's article."

WITH THE EXCEPTION of Devine's feature story on the Christmas Confessor, the day was uneventful. Jack had touched base with Max, who had found no information on Dwayne Franklin. Even more discouraging, none of Max's calls to the Elkton hotels had turned up anyone who remembered Boone Shaw.

Instead of babysitting Abby all day, Jack should have been handling the hotel questioning the old-fashioned way. On foot and in person.

Yet, he didn't trust anyone else to keep Abby safe, so here he stayed, holed up in the Don't Say a Word office.

When his cell phone rang late in the day, Jack expected the caller ID window to show Max's number. Sam Devine's name appeared in the small display screen instead.

Perfect timing. Jack had planned to share his thoughts on Devine's article in person, just as soon as Abby wrapped up her work day. But Devine launched into conversation before Jack had a chance to voice his opinions on the man's reporting skills.

"I've got something you need to see." Devine's excitement bubbled through the phone.

Jack had no patience for more of the man's scams. "Another card you put together? Speaking of which, where did you get the photo? From an old case file?"

The silent pause on the other end of the line confirmed Jack's guess wasn't far from the truth.

Devine stuck to his original topic as if Jack hadn't said a word. "You need to meet me. Same place as before. Half hour."

Jack glanced at his watch then at the hustle and bustle of the busy office. There were enough bodies here to keep Abby safe while he met with Devine. "I'll be there in fifteen."

A short while later he spotted Devine at the same table inside the mall. This time, Devine had cleared all but two chairs away.

Jack stood, scowling down at Devine. "This had better be good."

Devine brushed a lock of his hair from his face. Jack made the man nervous. Good.

Something akin to euphoria danced in Devine's eyes. "The article drew out your guy."

"Assuming you're telling me the truth, you've got my attention."

"He liked the piece."

"The piece?" Jack couldn't help himself. "Your piece is nothing but supposition and make-believe. You're lucky I don't have Hayes arrest you for interfering in an ongoing investigation."

"Seems to me this guy's delivering postcards faster than you can come up with leads."

Jack straightened defensively. "What was so important that I had to rush down here? I have better places to be."

"This." Devine patted the cell phone in his pocket. "He contacted me."

"Who?" Jack narrowed his eyes, impatience simmering inside him. He gestured for Devine to give him the phone. "You have no idea who we like for this, do you?"

But instead of backing down as Jack had expected, Devine stood, eyeing Jack head-on. "I know you've got three faces tacked to the board at the precinct."

Maybe the reporter had better sources than Jack had given him credit for. "But?"

"But the only suspect you need is the Christmas Confessor."

"Seems to me I've heard this story before."

Devine lowered his voice. "This time he sent a text message."

Jack held out his palm, trying to contain his disbelief but failing miserably.

Devine opened his cell, tapped the appropriate keys to pull up a message and handed the phone to Jack.

It's better to give than to receive.

Jack laughed. "I'm not so sure he liked your story."

"He likes his name, though." Devine reached for the phone, scrolled to the bottom of the message and handed the phone back to Jack.

Jack read the signature out loud. "Christmas Confessor." He checked the incoming caller ID and the blocked number. Then Jack shot Devine a glare. "Based on your track record, I'd say you sent this to yourself from an unlisted number."

Yet something about Devine was different. The last time they'd met, Devine had given off nonverbal clues that suggested he was lying. This time the only nonverbal cue the man emitted was his palpable excitement.

Someone had sent this text to the reporter as the result of the story, but who? Jack found it difficult to believe the killer would have let his fingers do the talking to Devine.

With the right resources, however, Jack could unlock the originating phone number in no time flat.

He moved to tuck Devine's phone into his pocket, but the other man pursed his lips and held out his hand. "Not so fast. No warrant. No phone."

Jack muttered a string of expletives beneath his breath,

then pushed away from the table, calling back to Devine as he walked away. "Leave that phone on. I'll be calling you to hand it over once the warrant's in my hand."

"HEY, NATALIE. What's your first reaction to this card?"

Abby had decided to feature special holiday blogs in order to lighten the severe mood she'd created online by publishing Melinda and Emma's postcards.

Abby walked to the lobby, staring at the postcard in her hand. "Natalie?"

Yet, nothing and nobody greeted her but an empty desk.

The office had emptied out as if someone had pulled the plug. The local news stations were forecasting snow by Christmas Eve and the last-minute shopping crunch was on.

Based on the way she could hear a clock ticking somewhere deep in the building, Abby would have to say most everyone had gone home early.

'Twas the season for shopping, after all.

Abby couldn't help but wonder where Jack had gone. He'd left to meet Devine over ninety minutes ago. Surely he should be back by now.

Dread wrapped its icy fingers around Abby's neck and squeezed.

"Natalie?"

Still no answer.

Natalie's chair sat empty, facing the wrong direction, as if she'd rushed away from the desk quickly. Furthermore, her coat and purse sat to the side of her desk, as if she'd been preparing to leave for the night, but had forgotten them in her rush to go…where?

Natalie's computer screen remained powered on, the option box for shutting down the system still blinking from the middle of the monitor's screen.

"Natalie?" Abby yelled out as loudly as she could.

Perhaps the young woman had decided to run one last check of the kitchen, making sure the appliances were switched off for the evening.

Abby hurried toward the kitchen. Empty darkness greeted her, matching the hollow sensation building inside her chest.

She blew out a sigh, bolstered herself and stepped back to the hallway.

"Natalie?"

The young woman had to be inside the office somewhere. She had to be.

Silence.

Nothing but silence.

Abby returned to the main desk, staring down at Natalie's purse and coat, but it was something altogether different that captured her focus.

She blinked, shifting her gaze to the desk, to the pile of mail Abby had asked Natalie to pick up earlier that afternoon.

One shiny postcard stood out from the pile, as if Natalie had slid it free to study the black-and-white photograph pasted to one side.

Bile rose in Abby's throat and she clasped a hand across her mouth.

She recognized the postcard's subject instantly. The blunt-cut hair. The fair coloring. The laughing smile.

The shot had been taken while the subject worked, obviously without her being aware she was being watched and photographed.

Abby slid her hand into one of her gloves before she turned over the card, not wanting to leave any prints.

Just like the others, this one had been labeled with a single sentence. The message brief, but effective.

It's better to give than to receive.

Tears clouded Abby's vision as she turned the card back over and reached for the phone.

Jack answered his cell on the first ring, at the same moment the reality of what Abby had found hit her full force, stealing her breath.

She choked on a terrified sob, unable to speak momentarily.

"Abby?" Concern and urgency tinged Jack's voice. "Where are you?"

"Natalie."

She forced the word from a throat clogged by emotion and fear, touching a gloved finger to the image of the young woman she'd grown to consider a friend.

"I found a postcard," she repeated, as a lone tear slid down one cheek.

"With Natalie?" Jack's voice climbed with uncertainty, as if he hadn't quite heard Abby correctly.

"Of Natalie." Abby leaned heavily against the desk, squeezing her eyes shut against the threatening tears. "She's gone, Jack. Gone."

"Are you alone?"

"Hurry, Jack."

"Don't move, and don't touch a thing."

THE CHRISTMAS CONFESSOR watched Abby Conroy's reaction from where he sat in his parked car. He enjoyed the mix of uncertainty, shock and fear that played across her pretty, know-it-all features almost as much as he enjoyed the Christmas carolers winding their way through the street.

A young man tapped on his window and waved. The Confessor waved back, mouthing the words, "Merry Christmas."

After all, it *was* a merry Christmas.

A *very* merry Christmas.

As far as the Confessor was concerned, the giving season was only now about to begin. Little did Abby Conroy know this year's festivities had been planned especially with her in mind.

The Confessor laughed as he watched Abby reach for the phone. He cranked on the car's ignition, knowing he had to get moving.

The woman was smart enough to realize the receptionist had been abducted, and no doubt the police would be here in full force any moment.

Much as he'd love to stay for the light show and the play of red and blue against red and green, he had things to do.

He stole a peek at the plaid blanket covering the receptionist's unconscious form on the backseat before he eased the car from its parking space along the curb.

Inside the building's reception area, Abby Conroy stood illuminated by the overhead lighting, arms wrapped tightly around her waist as she waited.

"Ho, ho, ho," the Confessor said under his breath.

The receptionist moaned and he forced his attention away from Abby Conroy and back to his driving.

Tonight, he vowed to give his full, undivided attention to the beauty in the backseat, but come tomorrow, he'd refocus on his ultimate target, his ultimate Christmas present.

Abby Conroy.

He had a feeling this Christmas would be his merriest yet.

Chapter Thirteen

Hours later, Jack led Abby through the door to their suite and pulled her into his arms. The protectiveness growing inside him during the past days had taken over every inch of his body, his thoughts, his plans.

During the on-site investigation and the questioning Abby had endured down at the police station afterward, she'd held herself together, kept her chin up, never wavered physically or emotionally. At least not that anyone would notice—anyone but Jack.

Jack, on the other hand, spotted the anger, tears and frustration lurking just below the surface of her control.

And the only thing he'd wanted to do for hours was this. He'd wanted to hold her, comfort her, wrap her up and shield her from the horror of whatever fate had befallen Natalie.

For Jack knew in his gut and heart that Natalie hadn't simply left her desk and walked away. She'd been taken. She'd been taken by whomever it was that had been sending the postcards, and she wasn't coming back.

The dread and certainty were so strong they threatened to overwhelm Jack, but he held the emotions at bay, compartmentalizing them, knowing his phone would ring the instant Hayes and his team caught a break...or found Natalie's body.

In the meantime, he'd hold Abby.

He pressed a kiss to her forehead, then to each eyelid, realizing he'd never felt such tenderness for another human being, not even for his younger sister.

Abby Conroy had reached deep inside his heart and taken hold. Even though Jack knew nothing would come of whatever it was that had happened between them, he decided to ride it out for tonight, for tomorrow, for however many days they had left together.

"I think she's already dead."

Abby whispered the words against his shirt as the first tear slid over her lashes and down her cheek.

Jack cupped her chin, staring into her frightened eyes. "Don't give up yet." He had no plans to tell her he'd given up the moment he'd stepped into the reception area and assessed the scene.

Years of investigative work did that to a man—to anyone.

Sometimes your instincts were wrong, but for Jack, they were usually right. He could only pray the distraction of falling for Abby had thrown off his judgment. Perhaps Natalie was safe somewhere right now. Safe. Unharmed. Alive.

Jack's gut protested otherwise.

"Stay with me, Jack." Abby tightened her arms around Jack's waist, her body pressed to his.

Heaviness descended over Jack as if he'd taken on a measure of Abby's heartache. He held her, thinking not of how much he wanted her, but rather of how much he wanted to comfort her.

So he did.

He hoisted Abby into his arms as if he'd done so countless times before. She anchored her arms around his neck and tucked her tear-streaked face against his chest, and he carried her through the suite and into her bedroom.

"I'll hold you until you fall asleep."

She shook her head then covered his mouth with hers, tenderly pressing her lips to his. "Stay."

Jack held her until she stopped crying, until her breathing went even and smooth and the tension slipped from the arm she'd tucked inside his arm, the legs she'd intertwined with his.

Then he reached for the blanket folded neatly at the bottom of the bed, tugging it up and over her sleeping form. He did so with every intention of slipping out of bed, planning to check on her periodically, listening in case she should call him during the night.

Instead, Jack did what Abby had asked him to do.

He stayed.

And although the reality of the danger lurking outside was as near as the door to the suite, Jack slept, deeply and soundly, tucked against Abby. Together.

He didn't move until his cell phone rang the next morning, jolting him awake. He squinted at the bedside clock then pushed away from Abby's still sleeping form.

"Rockford Park," Hayes said the instant Jack answered his phone.

"Natalie?" Jack stepped into the living area and pulled the bedroom door shut behind him.

"I've got two uniforms on their way to pick you up."

"How bad?"

"Let's just say you'll want to let Abby sit this one out."

JACK HAD WOKEN Abby, breaking the news to her gently. One uniformed officer had stayed at the inn, standing guard outside their suite. Sharron Segroves had agreed to sit with Abby, and had arrived bearing fresh coffee and a breakfast tray just as Jack and the second uniformed officer headed out.

Now Jack stood shoulder to shoulder with Tim Hayes, their shared resignation hanging heavy in the frigid winter air as they watched the investigative unit process the scene.

An early morning jogger had found Natalie's body, naked and wrapped in a fleece blanket bearing the imprint of a laughing Santa Claus. Still-intact store tags suggested the killer had purchased the blanket just for this use.

Jack knew what they'd find in the way of evidence. Nothing. Sure, they could question each and every cashier at the megastore from which the blanket had been bought, but assuming the killer had paid with cash, chances were slim anyone would remember a thing about him.

It was Christmas week, for crying out loud. Holiday shoppers didn't buy festive fleece blankets to wrap around murdered women, did they? Why would a cashier notice one person more than the next in the throng of frenzied shoppers?

It's better to give than to receive.

"Bastard." Jack's warm breath created a burst of steam, dissipating into the morning air.

The heavy, gray sky seemed to grow more menacing while he and Hayes stood their ground, waiting, watching.

"Got something." The technician processing Natalie's body waved and called out.

Jack and Hayes stood over him seconds later.

"Not sure what it is." The tech shook his head. "I've never seen anything like it."

But Jack had.

He flinched at the mutilated skin on Natalie's upper thigh.

"What do you think?" Hayes asked, his tone a mixture of anger and repulsion.

"Lips," Jack answered.

Their killer had escalated from sending snapshots of his old crimes to killing anew. Just in time for Christmas.

"Son of a bitch," Hayes said flatly. "Think this is your guy? Or my guy?"

"Looks like they're one and the same." Jack inhaled deeply of the frigid December air and shoved his hands deep inside his pocket. "Looks like his Christmas giving has begun."

"More like Christmas taking." Hayes turned to get out of the technician's way. "Damn shame."

Damn shame.

The words seemed too slight to sum up the tragic scene, the lifeless body of the young woman who just yesterday had chatted with Jack about her plans to travel north for the holidays to be with her family.

Damn shame.

For all of his years of experience, the overwhelming senselessness of murder still gripped Jack at every new crime scene. He pictured the case board back at Hayes's office and wondered how quickly they'd add Natalie's picture to the victim column.

Then Jack wondered who was waiting at home for the visit from Natalie that would never happen. Who had wrapped Christmas presents for the pretty, young blonde who would never open another present again?

Then Jack fell back on the tried and true, grimacing even as he repeated the too simple phrase, in full agreement with Hayes.

"Damn shame."

A HEAVY SILENCE hung in Jack's rental car as he and Abby headed south toward Elkton, Maryland.

Jack had returned to the inn expecting Abby to be inconsolable. Instead, he'd found her showered, dressed and armed with a mapped list of every hotel in the Elkton, Maryland, area.

Her reaction to the discovery of Natalie's body shouldn't

have surprised him. She was a woman of action—determined to help Jack and stop a killer from striking again.

"Another ten minutes should do it." Jack could see nothing more of Abby than the line of her jaw. She'd turned to look out her window at the start of their drive and she hadn't shifted positions since.

He recognized the posture, recognized the visible manifestation of defeat, grief and guilt.

"Not your fault," he said softly.

"Don't start with me, Jack. Not now."

The edge to Abby's voice was sharper than he'd expected, yet he was glad to hear the heat of anger tossed into her mix of emotions.

She'd survive. Of that, Jack had no doubt.

"When Emma died, I blamed myself for months."

His admission did the trick. Abby turned to face him, pale brows drawn together, a slight frown marring her beautiful features.

"You've blamed yourself for years, Jack. You're blaming yourself right now, aren't you?"

Of course he was. How could he not?

Jack nodded. "I'd like to tell you that time heals all wounds, but I've always found that line to be a load of crap."

He sneaked a glimpse at her, taking his eyes from the road for a split second, long enough to see the shimmer of moisture welling at the line of her lower lashes.

"Thanks." She tipped her head back against the seat, then dropped her focus to the map she'd prepared. "No one could ever accuse you of sugar-coating things." She pointed to the exit sign looming ahead. "This is us."

Jack and Hayes had come to the joint conclusion that every possible lead had to be pursued immediately. No more wondering what if, or theorizing about what might happen next.

The hypothetical had become the unthinkable.

They had a new victim on their hands and a killer on the loose.

Hayes had sent an officer to snap a photo of Dwayne Franklin with express instructions to get an identification from the photography shop as soon as possible. Sam Devine had been pulled in for questioning and a warrant was in the works for his phone and text messages.

Abby and Jack had planned a face-to-face hotel tour, complete with a stop-by-stop showing of Boone Shaw's photograph they hoped might unearth the information Max's phone call had not.

Hours later, they were just about to give up when an unmapped location caught Abby's eye.

"Pull over."

Jack slowed the car. "I thought we had another three blocks before our next turn."

Abby had twisted to look out the window behind her. "Bed-and-breakfasts, Jack. We never thought of smaller inns."

Sonofagun. Talk about an amateur mistake.

He pulled a U-turn, then eased the car into a parking space across the street from a turn-of-the-century home, complete with wide front porch and Welcome sign.

"Oh, sure," the older gentleman working the counter said with a nod of his head, "I can even tell you the guy's name. Boone. Never forget an unusual name like that. I'm a student of language, I'll have you know."

Abby nodded politely, but Jack wasted no time on niceties. They were racing against a ticking time bomb, and if Jack had anything to do about it, they'd figure out exactly who Boone Shaw had been tracking before anyone else died.

"Did he leave a forwarding address?" Jack asked.

The older gentleman looked at Jack over the top of his reading glasses, his annoyance palpable. "He left more than that."

"How so?"

"Well, he left an unpaid bill and a room full of personal belongings I've got no use for."

Jack's pulse kicked up a notch.

"Went out one day and never came back." The manager shrugged. "I suppose you'll be wanting to see his things, right? Like one of those crime shows on television?"

Jack spotted the twinkle in the man's eyes and played into the role. "You'd be doing our investigation a great service, sir."

"Got everything boxed up in the back. Follow me."

But after an exhaustive review of the box contents, Abby and Jack hadn't learned anything other than the name of the painkillers Boone Shaw took to ease his suffering and his preferred sock color.

They found no camera, no film and worst of all, no notes.

The manager promised to call if he thought of anything else, and Jack and Abby headed back toward Wilmington, hoping one of the other search angles had borne more fruit.

A dark, raw night had settled thoroughly over the region by the time they began their drive back, the atmosphere outside perfectly matching the mood inside their car.

Jack's cell rang just minutes south of the city.

With any luck at all, they were about to catch a break.

Heaven knew they needed one.

THE CHRISTMAS CONFESSOR moved stealthily through the apartment as if he'd been there countless times before. He laughed to himself as he took in the decorations, the framed photographs, all perfectly placed, perfectly planned, with no consideration given to how easily they could all be taken away…or destroyed.

The sound of water drifted into the apartment from the end of a hallway and he decided to wait, lowering himself to an overstuffed chair upholstered in an annoying pink-and-white garden-print fabric. Too old for a woman so young. Or on the other hand—he laughed—perfectly appropriate for someone at the end of her life. Whether she knew it or not.

He reached for the remote, feeling a surge of power as he gripped the object in his gloved hand. He powered on the television and chose the late-night news, smiling as the talking heads mentioned the mysterious appearance of postcards from someone dubbed the Christmas Confessor and the body of a young woman found in Rockford Park.

"Idiots," he murmured under his breath.

The media might think themselves brilliant for adopting the season-appropriate nickname, but they'd never find him. He did enjoy the attention, he had to admit. And why not? He was good at what he did.

Very good.

After all, he'd had a lot of practice.

And he was about to get even more.

The sound of water in the back of the apartment stopped abruptly and he muted the volume on the television, watching mindlessly as a female anchor did her best to report the day's sports.

What would it be like to snuff out the life of someone so well-known? She fit the profile. Aloof. Holier-than-thou. Female.

A door creaked at the other end of the apartment and he powered off the television, pushing to his feet.

He moved quickly to the doorway, pulling the cord from his pocket.

Then he waited, rewarded before long by the sound of the woman's off-key singing filtering down the hall as she approached.

In one swift motion he brought the cord over her head and around her throat as she moved past him. Her body tensed, her hands clawed at her throat, her fingers furiously dug at the cord now squeezing off her air supply.

And as he pushed her toward a large mirror on the wall, her terrified gaze found his, and he smiled.

The light of recognition and horror in her eyes filled him with a satisfaction even more deep and pure than his earlier murders had brought.

After all, Gina Grasso was about to take her last breath, live her last moment, think her last thought.

And the Christmas Confessor wanted to make sure his was the last face she saw.

Chapter Fourteen

"She's not answering either phone." Abby did her best to keep her fear and anxiety at bay, yet she couldn't deny the way her pulse rushed through her veins, kicked to a frenzy the moment Jack relayed the purpose of Devine's call.

They'd been less than five minutes south of Wilmington when the reporter had phoned Jack.

He'd gotten another message, this one on his hotel voice mail, leaving only a street address. A street address Abby knew as well as she knew her own.

Gina's.

"Do you think Devine's making this one up?" she asked, hope flickering then fading inside her.

Jack looked away momentarily, as if testing out the weight of her question. When he snapped his dark gaze back to Abby, he reached for her hand. "I'm calling Hayes. He can get there faster than we can."

"Do you still think Devine faked the third postcard?"

Jack nodded. "But I think the Confessor liked what Devine did. He's reaching out to him now. I believe he's telling the truth."

As much as Abby didn't want to give voice to her next thought, she felt compelled to do so. "What if we're already too late?"

Jack squeezed her hand, keeping her fingers firmly anchored inside his own. The kind gesture didn't go unnoticed or unappreciated. "We'll keep trying to reach her until we find her."

Yet the moment they reached Gina's apartment, Jack knew they were already too late.

The door to Gina's apartment sat slightly ajar, no more than an inch or two, but enough to let Jack know something was amiss. Once inside, reality pushed at the perimeter of his awareness.

Furniture visibly askew.

A mirror knocked from the wall and cracked.

The imperceptible presence of death, so familiar and yet so foreign each time he experienced the sensation. An eerie calm that was too still, too quiet, too devoid of life.

"Jack?" Abby moved to push past him, but he grabbed her arm, pulling her back and behind him.

They'd beaten the police somehow, and the last thing he wanted was for Abby to come face-to-face with her best friend's body...or the killer. "Stay here."

"Gina?" Abby's cry shattered the unnatural silence of the apartment.

Something creaked to the right and down the hallway and for a split second, Jack hoped they might not be too late.

Sam Devine emerged from a back bedroom, hand clasped over his mouth, face so pale he'd taken on a greenish hue.

Anger seethed inside Jack. "What in the hell are you doing here?"

But Devine never answered. He managed only to shake his head before he rushed into a small bathroom, the noise of his retching reaching them a moment later.

"Gina?" Abby cried out again just as footfalls pounded down the hall.

Tim Hayes's features shifted and tightened the moment he crossed the threshold, having no doubt taken the same visual inventory Jack had. His stare locked with Jack's. "How the hell did you two get here first?"

But Jack said nothing, reaching instead for Abby, wanting to protect her from this place, from whatever sight had evoked Devine's reaction, wanting to take her away forever.

"Bad?" Hayes asked.

Jack nodded. "We haven't gone back. Haven't touched anything, but Devine's in the bathroom."

"Devine?" Rage tangled with Hayes's disbelieving tone.

Jack nodded toward the bathroom door just as more retching sounded.

"So much for preserving the evidence trail," Hayes muttered.

Abby pulled against Jack, freeing her arm from his grasp. She broke free and raced down the hall ahead of the officers who had arrived on Hayes's heels.

"Abby!" Jack cried out, taking off in a sprint, wanting to spare her from the horror he knew waited at the end of the hall.

But by the time he reached her, he was too late.

Abby stood frozen in the doorway to Gina's bedroom. Gina lay sprawled naked across her bed, the cord still wrapped around her lifeless neck.

A card sat on her stomach, a black-and-white snapshot of Gina, laughing, a cruel juxtaposition of life to death.

The stench of burnt flesh registered just as Abby let loose with an eardrum splitting scream.

Jack pulled her into his arms, spinning her away from the sight of her best friend's body, murmuring soothing words of empty promises in her ears.

"He won't get away with this. We'll get him."

But would they? Would they ever stop the monster who'd come back to life here and now? In the days before Christmas? In the sleepy city of Wilmington, Delaware?

None of it made any sense. None of it.

The sound of Hayes telling one of the uniformed officers to hold Devine for questioning burst through the sense of numbness pervading Jack's every faculty. Hadn't he just seen Gina two days ago? Laughing. Alive.

In his arms, Abby sobbed, her screams now silent, her pain palpable. Another loss. Another tragic death. How many would she have to endure before Jack found this bastard and made him stop?

Devine.

Devine had known Gina was about to be murdered. He'd been here first. Had he wrung the life from her body himself? How far was the man willing to go to create a headline?

Jack broke away from Abby, slamming his full body weight into Devine as the reporter emerged from the bathroom, wiping his face with a washcloth. The force of Jack's assault knocked Devine backward into a shelving unit.

"You sonofabitch."

A crystal vase hit the floor and exploded. Then a frame slid sideways, also hitting the floor and shattering with a crash.

"I didn't kill her. I found her like this. I swear." Devine's voice was that of a scared, little boy. "I must have interrupted him. I never expected to find her here. He usually takes the bodies outside. To a park." He was babbling now, fear and shock tangling in his features.

"What did you expect to find?" Jack asked.

Devine shook his head. "I don't know. Maybe he was trying to set me up."

Jack couldn't care less. As far as he was concerned, Devine's article had kicked the killer into high gear. Two bodies in one day were two bodies too many. End of story.

Three faces stared back from the photo beneath the pulverized glass.

"You planted the Bricken postcard?" Jack asked.

Devine nodded. "I thought the cards were some sort of game. I wanted to build it into something more." He broke down sobbing.

"You expect us to believe that's all you did?" Hayes spoke from behind Jack.

"I never meant for anyone else to die." Devine hung his head, his body sagging beneath the weight of his confession.

Jack shoved the reporter aside, into the clutches of a uniformed officer.

Hayes reached for Jack's shoulder, offering a steadying support, locking stares until Jack reigned in his fury and got himself under control.

Jack's focus fell to the floor, landing on the shattered frame, the exposed photo.

Vicki. Gina. Abby.

The same shot Abby proudly displayed in her apartment.

Three friends for life. Alive. Happy. Together.

"And then there was one," the crime scene technician called out from the bedroom, where he'd begun processing the scene.

"Say again," Hayes called out.

"The card," the tech answered. "That's the message on the back. 'And then there was one.'"

Jack lifted his gaze from the photo of the three friends to Abby's frightened and shocked face.

And then there was one.

Jack Grant planned to do whatever it took to keep it that way.

ABBY SANK INTO her favorite chair and shut her eyes, willing away the shock and the horror, the loss and the emotional anguish of finding Gina brutally murdered, her body stripped naked and branded like a slab of meat.

After they'd finished with the police, Abby had asked Jack to take her home—home to her apartment, to the familiar, to memories of happier times. Much to her surprise, he'd agreed.

Yet nothing about the familiar of her apartment could wash away the images of Gina's brutal murder.

She'd been strangled, sexually assaulted and posed.

And then there was the postcard.

"Drink this." Jack's deep voice eased into Abby's consciousness, grounding her momentarily with his unwavering strength.

She opened her eyes, studied the steaming cup of what looked like tea in his hand and shook her head. "Can't."

He took one of her hands, tucked the warm cup inside then positioned her other hand to cradle the mug. "Try."

He dropped to his knees in front of her, his eyes displaying a concern so genuine it stole Abby's breath.

"Is this because of me?" She voiced the question even though she'd been doing her best to shove the thought deep down inside her mind.

"None of this is your fault." Jack reached to brush a strand of her hair behind her ear. He let his fingers linger against her cheek, his touch intimate and unexpected.

Abby didn't fight the contact, didn't shift away. If anything, she leaned into his strength and his warmth, hungry for his reassurance that everything would be all right. Praying for him to tell her Gina was alive and well. That today had been nothing more than a bad dream.

But she knew better.

Warm tears stung at the back of her eyelids.

Abby had fought against crying since the moment they'd stormed into Gina's apartment. Now she could no longer fight the need to cry, the need to release her pent-up grief and anger.

Her body went limp, as if she'd lost the will to fight against everything—her tears, the truth, the Christmas Confessor.

"Why?" She managed only a tired whisper, ashamed of the self-pity she heard in her voice, but speaking the words just the same. "Why Don't Say a Word? Why Natalie? Why Gina? What did I do to draw him to us?"

Jack brought his face close to hers, forcing her to meet his stare, to look at him as he answered her. "He's a madman, Abby. You can't force rationality on a madman."

"Was it the *People* feature?"

Robert had warned her against the publicity. He'd accused her of losing focus on what really mattered—their loyal readers, the loyal postcard senders.

He'd accused her of wanting the limelight, when nothing could have been further from the truth.

But now…now the limelight was so bright Abby felt blinded.

Jack frowned, the move creasing his forehead. "He might have seen an opportunity. Who knows?"

But Abby suddenly focused on a more frightening thought. "What if this had nothing to do with the article?"

Jack remained silent, studying her carefully, his brows drawing closer together.

"I think he knows me." Abby whispered the words and what little emotional control she had left broke.

Jack plucked the cup of tea from her hands, set it aside and pulled her into his arms in one motion. Sobs wracked her body as he held her, cradling her in his lap, stroking her hair, murmuring soothing words against the top of her head.

When his mouth found hers, she didn't fight him, relaxing into his kiss, into the sensation of his lips on hers, his tongue tasting, exploring, igniting the simmering heat inside her she could no longer ignore.

The need to lose herself with Jack pushed aside all of her fears and doubts, her questions, her anxieties. For a moment, she thought she might be able to hide from the world with Jack, lost in his loving embrace.

Then he broke contact, standing and walking across the room, leaving her colder than she'd been a few moments before.

WHAT IN THE hell was he doing? What was he thinking?

Jack forced himself to pull away from Abby, the soft curves of her body and the sweet taste of her mouth.

The woman had just lost her closest friend and was more than likely next on the killer's hit list and here he was, acting like a sex-crazed animal.

Sure, stress could do strange things to people, but Abby deserved better. Abby deserved his strength and his respect, not his sexual advances.

"Sorry." He spoke the apology gruffly as he moved away, putting as much distance between them as Abby's living room would allow.

Hot color marred Abby's fair cheeks.

Embarrassment? Desire?

He shook the question out of his mind.

The Christmas Confessor was moving closer and closer, escalating with each murder, and yet Jack had no earthly idea of who the man was.

There wasn't time to pursue the attraction between him

and Abby. There wasn't time to seek comfort in each other's arms, to make love with abandon if only for the moments of escape and pleasure their joining would provide.

The scene inside Gina's home confirmed that Shaw had not been her killer. No man riddled and weakened by cancer was capable of the violence they'd witnessed tonight.

Whoever had killed Gina had left her posed inside her apartment, breaking the usual pattern of taking the body to a public park. Chances were better than good that Sam Devine had interrupted the killer's routine. But then, the killer himself had allegedly called Devine, luring him to the address.

Detective Hayes had confirmed the muffled message on Devine's hotel voice mail, the caller's voice unrecognizable.

Why draw Devine and the authorities to the scene of the crime so quickly? Why?

What the hell was going on?

Jack needed to know who Shaw had been tracking. Find that name and they might have a prayer of stopping the killer before he killed again.

If only Shaw's personal belongings had yielded a clue, a name, a face. Anything.

I think he knows me.

Abby's words teased at the base of Jack's brain even as they sent a fresh wave of urgency through him. He'd thought the same thing himself a time or two since this journey had begun.

Could the killer be someone Abby knew?

Was familiarity the unknown factor that had triggered the first postcard? And what had set off the new Christmas killing spree after eleven years?

Had it been planned all along? Or had Devine's feature article pushed the Confessor to his breaking point?

The targets were growing more personal. Natalie. Gina.

But was that because what had started as a card sent to a random Web site for publicity had become a personal crusade in response to Abby's blogs? Or had the killer known Abby all along?

Jack ran the list of suspects through his mind once again and focused, shutting out the fact he'd just kissed Abby and longed to do so much more.

Boone Shaw. Sam Devine. Dwayne Franklin.

Each fit in some way and not in others.

What was Jack missing?

Abby murmured something incoherent and Jack turned to study her. She met his gaze with moist eyes, red-rimmed with grief and shock and fear.

"Say again?" He urged her, keeping his voice even, his tone gentle even as possible motives, next steps and scenarios spiraled through his brain.

"I made him mad," Abby said, her throat working and her features smoothing, recovering from her crying jag and the shock of his kiss.

"Mad?"

"I called him a crank." She pushed herself taller in the chair, sitting up straight as if new determination had infused her with strength. "I made him mad."

Jack thought back to the call from Melinda Simmons's father and the night Jack had first read Abby's blog. He hadn't read that first blog again, but probably should have.

What if Abby's words *had* triggered the killer to kill anew? What if he'd only meant to send the cards? To resurrect his notoriety?

Whoever the killer was, he was all about control. Of that, there was no doubt. Yet, Abby had called him a crank, not believing him to be a murderer. In effect, she'd publicly humiliated the man.

Hell, Abby's first response had made Jack angry back when he'd read it. What sort of an effect would it have had on the postcard sender himself?

Had the killer interpreted Abby's words as a dare? Had he felt the need to prove himself? Again. And again.

Jack had to start over from the beginning. He had to make sure he hadn't missed anything. And he had to read everything Abby had written through the killer's eyes, looking for triggers. Searching for clues.

"Jack?"

Jack had been so deep into his line of thought he hadn't heard a thing Abby had said.

He closed the space between them and took Abby's hand. "Let's go."

"Where?"

"Back to the inn. I need to reread your blogs."

"I can pull them up on the computer here."

"No." Jack shook his head, steering her away from the chair and toward the door.

Suddenly, he needed Abby to be anywhere but here. He'd let himself become distracted by her emotions, by her pain. He shouldn't have let her come back to the apartment.

If the killer had zeroed in on Abby and her world, her apartment was just as familiar to him as it was to Abby. For all Jack knew, the killer was waiting and watching, even now.

Jack needed to move Abby back to the inn, back to safety, and he needed to make sure no one followed them.

"The picture's gone."

Jack followed the line of Abby's focus, noting the empty spot on the shelf where the photo of the three friends had sat. "Are you sure you didn't move it?"

She frowned, shaking her head.

If someone had been inside her apartment and had taken the print, that was all the more reason to get Abby out of here, now.

He pulled her toward the door. "Move."

"Jack…" Confusion swam in her stare.

"No arguments, Abby."

He rushed her out the door, down the sidewalk and into the car.

Jack needed Abby tucked away somewhere safe.

Now.

HE WATCHED THEM move toward the car. The detective, so far out of his territory it wasn't funny, reaching toward Abby's back, then hesitating, as if knowing he had no right to be there, no right to touch her.

Anger churned in the Confessor's stomach, sending heat pumping through his veins along with a renewed determination to see through every step of his plan, every piece of his puzzle.

He'd stayed ahead of the detective and his paltry investigative skills so far.

Why should finishing the work he'd set out to do be any different?

Hell, the media had given him so much coverage lately, he was more famous now than he'd ever been.

The Christmas Confessor.

He laughed.

He'd make Abby Conroy pay for ignoring him, just as he'd made the other women pay. Every last one of them.

By the time Christmas arrived this year, no one would ever ignore him again.

And Christmas *was* coming.

There was nothing more the Confessor loved than the joy of giving…over and over and over again.

"Ho, ho, ho," he muttered into the cold night air seeping in through the open driver's side window.

The taillights of the detective's rental car illuminated as the sedan eased away from the curb and headed down the street.

Then the Confessor cranked on the ignition of his own car, pulled away from the curb, and followed.

Chapter Fifteen

Abby didn't ask Jack to stay with her that night. Instead, she paced the small bedroom, from end to end, back and forth and back again.

She'd racked her brain trying to remember what she'd done with the photo of Vicki and Gina and herself. Tears threatened again and she blinked them back. She was done crying.

Jack was right. They were out of time. The only thing Abby had time for now was thinking. She was missing something and she knew it. Somewhere buried in her brain was a memory, a face, a word that would snap all of the puzzle pieces together.

She knew the killer.

She'd never been more sure of anything.

Sure, the man might not be a good friend, but at some point, they'd met. The attacks were too personal for him to be a stranger angered because he'd sent a postcard and she'd called him a crank.

Could Dwayne be the Christmas Confessor?

She pictured his outburst, his rare display of violence, but shoved the idea out of her head. It wasn't possible. It couldn't be.

He knew her well enough, certainly, and he followed the blog, but a killer?

There had to be someone else.

"Think, Abby. Think."

When she grew weary of pacing, she sat down on the bed. Fatigue pushed at the edges of her consciousness, but she fought against it, not wanting to sleep, not wanting to do anything but solve the puzzle.

No, that was a lie.

She'd wanted something far different from sleep earlier.

She'd wanted Jack, but he'd pushed her away. He'd given her glimpses of the emotion lurking beneath his tough shell and she'd thought perhaps she'd finally broken through.

For a fleeting moment, she'd fantasized about loving him and being loved in return. Then he'd caught himself, shut down his heart and pushed her away.

His expression and body language had shifted so abruptly from sensual and caring to the all-business, intense detective who had first shown up at the office that he'd left her speechless.

Part of her had wanted to pound her fists against his chest. Part of her had wanted to dare him to feel something. To be with her.

But instead, she'd had her own shut down, isolating herself, in the bedroom. Alone.

Alone.

She hated the word, but it was her reality. Abby was alone now. Robert was the only friend she had left.

She looked at the clock and decided it was too late to call him, even though she knew he wouldn't mind the intrusion into his sleep. She wondered if he knew about Gina.

Then Abby let herself lean back against the pile of pillows. She'd shut her eyes for just a minute, then she'd be recharged, ready to figure out what in the hell was going on.

She blinked her eyes shut, amazed at how heavy her lids felt.

Then she drifted, telling herself she'd rest only for a minute.

A minute.

Then Abby slipped into a deep, exhausted sleep.

JACK SPENT THE next day fielding calls, working through the pieces of the puzzle, waiting for Abby to wake up.

He'd heard her pacing during the night, until the wee hours of the morning. He'd checked on her a bit after four-thirty in the morning and had found her sound asleep.

He'd tucked her under the covers, regretting his decision to push her away even as he let his hand linger along the soft curve of her cheek.

She'd lost a coworker and her best friend in one day.

Jack couldn't help but wonder how much more she'd be able to take before she broke.

The winter sun was already beginning to set, dinnertime was approaching and Abby still hadn't awakened. Jack had checked on her again, as had Sharron Segroves. She appeared fine, other than being completely exhausted emotionally and physically.

Sleep was what her body needed, what Abby needed, in order to face the long road of grief and recovery ahead.

Jack's cell rang and he grabbed it on the first ring, not wanting the shrill noise to wake Abby.

"Two things." Tim Hayes's voice traveled across the line. "Got the positive ID on your favorite guy."

"Franklin?"

"You bet. Shop owner recognized his photo instantly. There's just one problem. We can't seem to find Franklin."

"Did you search his place?"

"Don't want to compromise evidence. Waiting on a warrant."

Another damned warrant. Jack groaned inwardly.

"We did, however, get the warrant on Devine," Hayes said. "Thought you might like to ride along."

"Wouldn't miss it."

"I'm headed over to his hotel in about an hour."

"I'll meet you at the station. Can I get an officer over here for Abby?" He'd been worried for her safety before, but now that he knew Dwayne Franklin was in the wind, he wanted someone with Abby at all times.

"Consider it done."

Perfect. An hour would give Jack time to eat and head out. And with a uniformed officer in place with Abby, he would know she was safe.

With any luck at all, by the time Abby awoke from her slumber, Jack would be able to tell her they were one step closer to ending the nightmare.

HE WATCHED HIS target, letting his mind wander while he waited to make his move.

The Confessor knew his past and his present were beneficial to some people—people who prayed on the curiosity of the public. People who craved the written word, who expressed themselves at the expense of their subjects.

There were some people, like Abby Conroy, who felt words could heal, words could soothe.

The Confessor knew the only thing words were good for were leaving messages.

And he knew the content of his next message just as surely as he knew exactly how he was going to take the next victim's life.

Actions.

Those were the things that really mattered, the things that could alter the path of a life…or end it.

There was nothing like watching the life drain out of a victim's face. Nothing like watching the glow of living leave their eyes, their flesh, their strength.

Similarly, there was nothing like the satisfaction of knowing a job had been well done. Nothing like leaving his mark, a message…yes…but also an action.

The Confessor prided himself on actions of control, of power, a reminder to others to watch and listen and learn.

The truth was no one knew when the Confessor would act next, kill next, mark next.

He patted his pocket, feeling the stiffness of the postcard. *This one's for you.*

The card was ready to be delivered, complete with message and photograph.

There was just one detail to be taken care of first. One life to be ended.

He watched the target move behind the window of the hotel room, his next victim's silhouette clear and sharp against the room's sheer curtains.

It never ceased to amaze the Confessor how surprised each of his victims were to see him. As if they never imagined someone might want them dead.

The Confessor pulled on his gloves and stepped forward, sure in his movement, his purpose.

Action.

Then words.

He was about to kill as he'd never killed before, yet he had no second thoughts, no doubts.

After all, he was a man with a purpose. A man with a message.

And the action he was about to take would surely drive that message home.

Action.

Then words.

Life really was simple if only people would take the time to pay attention.

ABBY COULDN'T BELIEVE she'd slept all day, and once she'd found Jack's note she'd done two things.

Ask the officer to move to a more discreet post and then go eat.

Sharron and Harold had said they'd help keep an eye out for strangers, and Abby had returned to the room, waiting for Jack to check in.

The officer had assured Abby he could watch the entrance to her room as effectively from his cruiser as he could from the door. Abby had thanked him, happy to have the security of his presence, but not wanting to do anything to jeopardize the inn's holiday business. Surely an armed officer standing guard didn't do much to keep the Christmas spirit alive.

Abby felt safe, and safe was something she hadn't felt since she found the postcard of herself on her kitchen window.

A chill danced down her spine. Every other postcard coincided with a murder. Why not hers? Had Jack's presence in her home saved her life?

She groaned and shook her head. Her life had forever changed during the past few days. Natalie and Gina were gone, lost to the ruthlessness of a madman. Don't Say a Word was forever tainted. If she were smart, she'd shut down the site forever.

But what about the true confessors? The growing numbers of postcard senders for whom confession truly was good for the soul? The estranged siblings for whom it was too late to say goodbye. The parent and child who would never be able to say they were sorry. The child who had cheated her way through college, deceiving everyone she knew.

Abby wasn't saying that their secrets were excusable, but for the most part, they were forgivable.

But not the Christmas Confessor.

His sins were neither excusable nor forgivable.

Anger swelled inside her and a sudden compulsion to write overcame her. Words and phrases filled her mind and she scrambled to get to her laptop, pressing the button to bring the computer out of standby.

The moment her word processing screen blinked to life, she began to type, words filling the screen, fingers flying on the keyboard.

She wasn't about to let some faceless killer intimidate her or shut down her site. She'd be damned if she'd sit idly by and not fight back. Jack knew how to investigate, how to track criminals, how to process facts and evidence. Abby knew how to write, how to express herself, how to blog.

And so she wrote, rereading the piece when she was done and changing not a single word. Her anger and de-termination and grief were there for anyone and everyone to read.

She went through the necessary steps to get online and into the management area for her Web site, then she hit Publish, hoping the words she'd written might convince a madman to stop, but knowing they'd probably achieve nothing at all, nothing but making herself feel heard. Right now feeling heard was the first step to taking her life back.

Abby posted the blog, gave it one more read to make sure she hadn't missed any typos, then sat back against the desk's chair. Satisfaction filled her, the feeling fleeting. Reality pushed at the edges of her sense of accomplishment, a reminder that Natalie was gone, Gina had been murdered, and their killer walked free regardless of how soundly Abby had condemned his actions, his thinking, his right to go on breathing.

The sound of the suite's entrance door clicking shut startled her from her thoughts.

"Jack?"

No answer.

A floorboard creaked and Abby's chest constricted. She scanned the surfaces of her room, looking for her cell phone, but not spotting it anywhere. She lifted the desk's phone receiver very carefully, just as another floorboard creaked, this one much closer to the entryway to her room.

"Jack?" she asked again, her mind racing as she searched for the button for the front desk and pushed out of the chair, moving toward the wall and away from the door.

"Abby?"

The sound of her name startled her, but the voice which spoke left her speechless.

Dwayne.

He cleared the doorway in one step, one arm behind his back, hiding…what?

Bright color flushed his cheeks and his eyes shone like those of a man possessed.

Had Jack been right all along? Was her neighbor a monster? A killer capable of taking the lives of Gina and Natalie and countless others?

"I missed you," he said flatly, as if it were normal for him to have tracked her here and found his way into her locked hotel room.

Abby's pulse raced so quickly the blood rushed in her ears. "How did you get in?"

"Were you calling someone?" Dwayne ignored her

question, nodded to the receiver in her hand, still keeping his own hand behind his back.

Abby shook her head. "Detective Grant wanted to let me know he'd be here in five minutes."

Dwayne's eyebrows lifted. "I didn't hear the phone ring."

Abby shrugged, unable to counter that particular observation.

Dwayne's expression shifted from gentle to ice-cold in the blink of an eye. "Hang up."

"He already hung up," Abby lied.

"Hang up," he repeated.

Abby replaced the receiver without looking, refusing to take her eyes from Dwayne and whatever it was he held behind his back.

"How did you find me, Dwayne?"

"I followed you."

Jack had been right. They never should have gone back to her apartment after they left the scene of Gina's murder. Yet that had been almost twenty-four hours ago.

"From where?" she asked, trying to keep her tone non-threatening.

"Your house. Where you belong." Dwayne's features darkened, and his tone dropped low and intent. "It's not right for you to be here…with him."

"He's protecting me, Dwayne."

Dwayne patted his chest with his empty hand, taking two steps toward Abby. "I protect you."

Abby backed away from him instinctively, stopping only when her back hit the curtained window behind her.

"I know you do, Dwayne. And I appreciate that, but Jack's a police officer. He's keeping me safe while he investigates the man who's sending the postcards."

Dwayne took another step toward her, and Abby

scanned the room for any object she could use as weapon of defense. Nothing. The only possible weapon—a reading lamp—sat too far away to reach.

"You need to come home with me, Abby. Where you belong."

Dwayne moved closer, just as Abby's cell phone rang from the suite's sitting room.

Then Dwayne made his move, swinging his concealed arm out from behind his back.

JACK DIALED ABBY'S cell as he pulled into the parking lot. When she didn't answer his mind began to run the possibilities. She was taking a shower, on another call, or the unthinkable had happened.

Yet, the unthinkable had already happened once today, and Jack wanted to be the one to tell Abby.

He'd spent the last hour debriefing with Hayes and his department.

Sam Devine had been murdered. They'd found him in his hotel room, strangled in the same manner as Natalie and Gina, yet he'd been fully clothed and unbranded.

His murder had served a purpose, not a need.

The killer had left behind a card. A photo of Abby taken outside Gina's apartment building, as if the killer intended to use Devine exactly as Devine had used him.

To tell a story.

This one's for you.

Had the killer taken Devine's life as a favor to Abby? Or as a favor to the investigators on the case?

The local police hadn't had any luck as far as originating numbers went for both Devine's text and voice mail messages. Both calls traced back to city payphones, located at opposite ends of the city. Local? Yes. Helpful investigative information? Not exactly.

Devine's luck had run out. The guy would no doubt love the headline his murder would inspire, but Jack was sure he'd rather be remembered for his name in the byline instead of the subject line.

Jack scanned the parking lot. And frowned when he spotted the officer's silhouette, sitting in the driver's seat of the police cruiser.

Jack launched himself from his car and crossed the lot, pounding on the officer's window.

"What the hell are you doing here instead of by her door?"

"She insisted," the officer answered.

"And you listened?"

Unbelievable.

Jack hurried across the lot, dialing Abby's cell phone as he moved.

Sharron Segroves stood searching one of her service carts, unaware of Jack's approach.

"Evening," he said, startling her. "How is she?"

Sharron twisted up her face. "That is one stubborn young woman. Harold and I have been keeping an eye on her room. No one in or out."

Jack supposed that was some sort of comfort, but it didn't mean something hadn't gone wrong, it didn't mean the gnawing pit of dread at the base of Jack's stomach had exploded to life for no reason.

Sharron Segroves returned her focus to her cart, flipping through the fresh towels she delivered each evening.

"Something wrong?" Jack asked, shifting his own focus to the windows of his suite. One silhouette moved against the window. Abby was in her bedroom. But why was she standing pressed to the window?

"I can't seem to find the master key," Segroves said distractedly. "I can't imagine where I put it."

But as a second silhouette moved into view inside Abby's room, Jack knew exactly what had happened to the key. He sprang into motion and tossed Sharron his phone. "Call 9-1-1. Now."

He never heard Sharron Segroves's response.

He heard nothing but Abby. Screaming.

DWAYNE SWUNG HIS concealed arm forward and Abby launched herself into motion, moving sideways. She was boxing herself into a corner, but had no other way of keeping space between her and the steadily approaching Dwayne Franklin.

Dwayne clutched a stack of papers in his fist. Envelopes. Abby blinked.

"You forgot your mail." He scowled. "There's no need to scream at me."

Abby's head spun with disbelief. "You followed me to give me my mail?"

Franklin's eyes went cold, void of expression. "It upsets me when you forget your mail. What if someone needs you?"

Abby's mouth went bone dry. She tried to swallow, but couldn't. Where in the hell was Jack?

As if on cue, the Arizona detective crashed into the suite, dipping his shoulder as he charged Dwayne, dropping the other man to the floor in one swift move.

"Get out," Jack barked at Abby. "Move to the other room. Now!"

She scrambled over the bed, not questioning, just doing as Jack wanted.

"I brought her mail," Dwayne mumbled as Jack pulled the big man's hands and feet up behind him, holding him immobile as sirens wailed in the distance, drawing steadily nearer.

"He brought my mail." Abby realized how inane the words sounded, but suddenly every word sounded inane, every reality surreal. What in the hell had just happened?

"He taped the card to your window, Abby." Jack leaned close to snarl in Dwayne's ear. "I want to know why."

"Because I love her." Dwayne's voice had gone soft, the voice of a frightened child.

"Jack." Abby stayed on the other side of the doorway, wanting to stay out of Jack's way. "He's not the killer. I know he's not."

"No." Jack shook his head. "I think he'd just a stalker and you're his lucky victim." He looked at Abby, pinning her with a glare so angry she sucked in a breath. "Devine's been murdered, so it appears we're out of options."

Abby staggered backward. "Murdered?"

Jack nodded. "And the Confessor left another card."

"Who?" Abby regretted the question even as she asked it. Suddenly, she didn't want to know.

"You, Abby." Jack's anger morphed to concern. "You."

Chapter Sixteen

The search of Dwayne Franklin's apartment turned up nothing that tied him to the murders. No cord. No branding tool. Nothing but evidence of a stalker's obsession with his victim—over two hundred black-and-white photographs plastered across Franklin's bedroom walls and ceiling.

All printed on the telltale specialty paper.

All taken from Franklin's side window, a perfect view of Abby's apartment and kitchen.

Jack had refused Abby's request to see the room. Seeing it had left him with an ice-cold chill in his veins. As far as he was concerned, Abby was better off not knowing what kind of madness had lived next door to her.

During the intake process, Franklin had admitted to living next door to Abby under an assumed name, living off of cash provided by his wealthy Massachusetts family. Turned out his family abhorred scandal, and Franklin's obsession with a woman outside of Natick hadn't fit the family plan. They'd paid off the victim and sent the disturbed son out of state…where he'd fixated on Abby.

Lucky her.

Franklin had followed Jack and Abby to the inn, waiting until he could make his move, lifting Sharron Segroves's master key and slipping past the officer on duty unnoticed. The officer had been reprimanded and assigned to his desk until further notice.

Who knew what might have happened had Jack not arrived when he did.

Jack was so angry he was of a mind to head north with the sole purpose of giving Franklin's family a lecture in ethics, but he had more pressing commitments. Like keeping Abby alive.

They sat inside the break room at the precinct with Hayes and two other officers, talking about exactly how they planned to do just that.

"You've got to move her," Hayes said. "The inn location is compromised."

Abby squeezed her eyes shut, the lines of fatigue and stress evident once again, bracketing her pale eyes. "Why don't you just lock me up?"

Her sarcasm wasn't lost on Jack, but Hayes actually nodded as though he might consider the idea.

"What I'd like to do now is go to my office." Abby pushed to her feet as she spoke. "I'm sure that if Jack stays with me or one of you kind officers sits beside me, I'll be safe. I need a change of scenery and I need to *work*."

The urgency in her voice reached inside Jack and twisted his gut.

Hayes shot Jack an incredulous glare. "Is she kidding?"

Jack held out a hand just as his phone rang.

He read the display panel on his phone and straightened. The Elkton bed-and-breakfast.

"Yes, sir?" Jack pushed away from the table and stepped outside the room.

"Found something inside a drawer that I missed before."

Jack's blood pumped a bit more quickly. "Such as?"

"Looks like a family photo to me, but the one man is definitely your Mr. Boone Shaw."

Family?

"How many people in the photo sir?"

"Three." The line fell silent while the manager apparently admired the shot.

"Sir?" Jack urged.

"Looks to be the Mr. and Mrs. and their son."

But the Shaws hadn't had any children. Could this be the mystery person for whom Boone Shaw had traveled cross-country?

"Thought you might like to come on down and take a look," the manager continued.

Much as Jack would love to, he needed to stay close to Abby. She had a reckless light in her eye that suggested she was close to her breaking point. In his experience a crime victim either shut down or fought back.

Abby Conroy was definitely a candidate for the latter, and if she fought back against the Confessor, chances were she'd lose.

For all Jack knew, that was the reason she'd developed the sudden urge to get back to work. Maybe Abby thought she could draw the Confessor out, expose him and end his killing spree.

She was probably right. But was Jack willing to take that risk in order to get his man once and for all?

He refocused on his phone call.

How could he get his hands on the photograph and stay close to Abby?

"Do you have a fax machine, sir?"

"Surely do." Another pause. "I also have one of those printers that can scan in a picture and e-mail it, want me to try that?"

Bingo. Jack nodded, then realized the gentleman had no way of seeing him.

"I'm at the local precinct sir, let me get an e-mail address for you to use."

"How exciting."

Jack had to smile at the enthusiasm in the manager's voice. He could only hope the newly found piece of evidence would be worth the wait.

ABBY FELT AS though she was about to crawl out of her skin.

Frustration and determination tangled inside her. If the Confessor wanted her so badly, let him come after her. Let him put himself out in the open where Jack and the local police could take care of him once and for all.

She'd go to the office. She'd let an officer go along with her, protecting her every step of the way.

And she'd call Robert.

She needed to know he was safe. Needed to let him know just how quickly things had escalated.

They were the only two friends left now, as surreal as it was to think about Gina being gone.

Abby thought quickly about her parents, thankful they were out of the country on their annual holiday cruise, but knowing how devastated they'd be when they arrived home to news of all that had happened during their absence.

She refocused, more determined than ever to put an end to this mess.

They needed answers. The victims needed justice. And Jack needed peace.

As far as Abby was concerned, she was the key to all three.

The nightmare had started at Don't Say a Word. With any luck at all, it would end there. Then Jack and the other families would have closure. They'd finally have the justice they'd been awaiting for the past eleven years.

Jack popped his head inside the room and gestured to Hayes.

"E-mail address?" Jack asked.

Hayes scribbled something on a scrap of paper and handed it to Jack. A moment later, Jack was back at the table, a hopeful light in his eye.

He reached across the table and squeezed Abby's hand. "The bed-and-breakfast manager found a photo."

"Of Shaw?" Abby straightened, feeling hopeful for the first time all day.

Jack nodded. "Shaw, his wife and a young man. Now we just have to hope the manager can figure out how to scan the image and e-mail it. He said he's never tried before."

Abby reached for Jack, her fingers brushing against his sleeve. "Let me go to the office. Send protection and I promise—" she held up a hand "—I will let the officer stick to me like glue. No arguments."

He searched her face before he answered. "You can't catch him by yourself, Abby."

Jack understood her better than she understood herself, Abby realized. The warning in his look rang crystal clear.

"I'm done waiting." Emotion choked her voice as she spoke.

Jack scrubbed a hand across his face, visibly torn between going with Abby and waiting for the photograph.

Jack turned to Hayes. "All right if I borrow one of your guys to go with Abby?"

Hayes nodded, pointing to the younger of the two officers. "Jones will stay with you."

"Thanks."

Abby headed toward the door and Jack followed, squeezing her elbow as she passed. "If Jones tells you to clear out for any reason, you clear out. Understood?"

She thought about telling him she didn't appreciate his tone of voice, but Abby knew Jack barked out orders because he cared about her.

Theirs might be a relationship born out of the pressures of the investigation and a chemistry neither could deny, but what they shared *was* a relationship.

And Abby couldn't help but wonder where it would lead if given a chance.

She touched her fingers lightly to his cheek. "Thanks. Call me as soon as you know something?"

He nodded, the hard lines of his face softening. "Will do. And I'll be there as soon as I can."

OUT OF HABIT, Abby headed straight for the kitchen and the coffeemaker as soon as officer Jones gave the office a walk-through. She and Jack had spent the most of the afternoon at the police precinct and the office had emptied out for the day.

"Be right back," she called out over her shoulder to the young officer who now stood guard at the door.

She shivered as she passed Natalie's desk, unable to wrap her brain around the fact she'd never see the young woman again. So many lives had shifted forever during the past few days. She could only hope the Christmas terror would soon end with the killer behind bars.

"Hey."

Robert's voice startled her just as she powered on the machine.

"Were you in the office?" Abby had called him on her way over, but had only gotten his voice mail.

He nodded. "Heard you come in, but I was on the phone with Gina's mother. I wanted to see what I could do to help with arrangements."

Abby winced. She'd been so wrapped up in her own world she hadn't called Mrs. Grasso to offer condolences.

"How are you holding up?" Robert's tone was more abrupt than usual, but she found solace in the friendship reflected in his eyes.

He pulled her into a hug and Abby welcomed her old friend's embrace.

"I was just about to put on coffee, unless you picked up extra on your way in today."

He usually did. Robert was reliable that way.

When he pushed her out to arm's length, the look of detachment in his gaze was one Abby had never seen there before. "You all right?"

He ignored her question, saying only, "You'd like that, wouldn't you?"

"What?" Her pulse quickened inexplicably.

Too much pressure, too many recent shocks to the system, no doubt. For both of them. Robert looked as shell-shocked as Abby felt.

"Coffee," he answered, his gaze darkening. "You'd like that if I brought you coffee. But do you ever bring me coffee?"

Abby turned to face him head-on. "Robert?" What was he talking about? She'd brought him coffee on countless occasions.

"You never say thank-you. You never say much at all, not unless it suits you in some way. You and Gina and Vicki were always like that."

Abby moved toward him, reaching for her friend's arm, shock sliding through her when he turned sharply away from her attempted touch.

Grief. He was reeling from the horrific shock of Gina's murder, surely.

"Let's go sit down."

But Robert had already stepped out of the kitchen, heading for their workspace.

Abby followed, but even as she did so, her insides

churned. What was going on? Where was the calm, collected Robert she knew so well?

As they headed back through the reception area toward their office, Abby realized Officer Jones was nowhere to be found.

"Did you see the officer who came over with me?"

A tight smile crossed Robert's face. "I suppose we'll have to hire you a bodyguard soon, right?"

She shook her head. "With any luck at all, this will all be over soon."

"Hopefully you'll get your wish."

Something darkened in Robert's gaze and Abby realized she wasn't the only one who'd lost a friend and a coworker this week. She wasn't the only one whose business had been terrorized by the Christmas Confessor.

Robert took a backward step and pointed to the door. "I did meet Officer Jones. He ran next door for doughnuts."

"Oh." Surprise and shock filtered through Abby. Not exactly a move she would have expected the young officer to make. Jack and Hayes would have his head.

Abby was struggling between forcing a smile for Robert and trying to process his rapid mood swings when she spotted a photo of her with Gina and Vicki sitting on Robert's desk.

Her photo.

The photo missing from her apartment.

"You have my picture."

Robert frowned, his features turning severe, rage glimmering in his eyes. "You didn't even thank me for fixing the glass."

"You were in my house?" She swallowed down the sudden tightness in her throat.

"So many times I've lost count. Some nights I stop by just to watch you sleep."

A wave of dizziness and shock crashed through Abby

as she looked at Robert with new eyes, listened to him as if hearing him for the first time, and realized Jack's gut about Robert might have been correct from the start.

Dread seized her gut and twisted. "Where is Officer Jones?"

Robert stepped close, his tone and demeanor threatening. "Exactly where he needs to be."

JACK HAD THOUGHT the e-mail image would never come through. The manager and his wife had made three attempts and after twenty minutes spent on the phone with the precinct's computer whiz, the third image appeared in Hayes's inbox.

The image had obviously been scanned from a worn photograph, cracked and faded with age. The shot had captured three people, just as the manager had described.

Boone Shaw stood with his arm around a woman Jack imagined to be his wife. A third person—a young man probably in his late teens or early twenties—stood slightly to the side of Shaw, as if he weren't entirely comfortable being included in the shot.

Then Jack noticed the similarity. The defiant set of the young man's jaw. The narrowed eyes Jack had seen recently…here…in Wilmington.

"Sonofa—"

Jack placed his fingers around the young man's image to block his hair, almost shoulder-length in the photo.

The likeness was uncanny. And suddenly Jack had every reason to believe his gut dislike of the man had been spot-on.

The memory of Abby's words rang through his mind.

We've been together since grade school with the exception of the year after Robert's father died.

How old was Robert Walker in the picture with the Shaws? Seventeen? Eighteen?

Had he been in New Mexico at the time of the murders?

He snapped open his phone and called the bed-and-breakfast manager, thanking the man for his help and his time.

"One other question?" A haze of urgency gripped Jack, sharpening his senses, his awareness of the fact Abby might be in grave danger even as he spoke. "Was there a date on that photo?"

"No," the older man said. "But it's the darnedest thing, we had to take it off of the card in order to get the computer to give us a good scan."

Jack reached for a nearby desk and gripped the corner. "Card?"

"Christmas card. The photo was glued to the front. Didn't I mention that?"

A split second later, Jack was in motion, racing for the exit. "It's Walker. It has to be Walker. And I just let her head to the office."

What a fool he'd been. And now he'd failed to protect Abby just as he'd failed to protect Emma.

Hayes scowled, holding his phone to his ear as he scrambled to catch up to Jack. "No answer."

"Jones?" Jack's sense that Abby's time was running out ratcheted to the next level.

Hayes nodded. "Not good."

"How far from here to there?" Jack asked.

"Fifteen minutes. Ten if we fly."

"Then we fly."

Jack broke into a dead sprint at the same moment Hayes called for backup.

As far as Jack was concerned, none of them would be able to cover the ground between the precinct and Abby's office fast enough.

And he'd let her walk right into the killer's web.

SHE PULLED HER phone from her pocket, dialing Jack's number from heart. She needed him here, and she needed him now.

"What are you doing?" Robert spun on her, slapping away the phone with a force that shot the small object from her hands.

Fury shone in his eyes. Had he gone mad?

"I was calling Jack." Abby dropped to her knees and scrambled toward Robert's desk, reaching beneath a partially opened desk drawer for her phone. She could barely make out the tiny square of metallic red beneath the bulk of Robert's desk.

"Don't move."

The unforgiving tone of Robert's voice froze Abby to the spot.

"He's a good man, Robert. He can help you. Let me call him."

Robert answered with a shove, slamming Abby's shoulder into the sharp edge of the open desk drawer.

"I'm a good man, Abby. Pay attention to me." He patted his chest. "Have you once asked me how I feel about everything that's happened?"

Abby's mouth had gone so dry she wasn't sure she'd be able to form words, but she did. "How do you feel, Robert?"

He leaned close, the anger in his eyes morphing to amusement. "I'm having the time of my life. You were right, you know. Confession is good for the soul."

Raw fear tore at her insides, sending a shudder through her entire body as she looked at him. "What are you talking about, Robert?"

He laughed, the sound sharp and bitter. "I'm talking about the fact I haven't had this much fun since I went to stay with my Uncle Boone in New Mexico."

Abby rocked back on her heels, barely able to sit. "New Mexico?" She'd known he'd gone out west somewhere during high school, but New Mexico?

Robert blew out a disgusted breath. "My mother couldn't wait to be rid of me once my dad died, and Boone Shaw supposedly owed my dad for once saving his life or some bull like that. As I remember it, you barely knew I was gone. You and the girls were so wrapped up with your little popularity contests."

His words stung, but he was right. She had been self-absorbed back in high school, and she hadn't kept in touch during the time he was gone. But Boone Shaw? Robert had known Boone Shaw?

"You worked with him?" Her head swam. "Did you know the victims? Why didn't you say anything?"

Robert clucked his tongue. "You're typically not this obtuse, Abby. Honestly, I'm a bit disappointed."

She tried to remember exactly what Jack had said about the photo found in Boone Shaw's room. *Shaw, his wife and a young man.*

Robert? Had Robert been the person Shaw had traveled cross-country to find?

"What did you do, Robert?"

"To whom?"

He towered over her, his expression menacing. Abby reached for his desktop to pull herself to her feet. One file drawer sat partially open and she wrapped her fingers around the top of the drawer, seeking leverage to pull herself up.

An object shoved down between the vertical files stopped her heart cold.

A tool. Wooden handle. Metal point.

She'd never seen the object in Robert's possession in all of the times she'd gone into his desk for records or billing statements.

"I'm trying to decide if you deserve an eye…or a pair of lips. Maybe both."

Robert's voice dropped so low and cold, Abby's mouth went dry. The quickened rhythm of her heartbeat vibrated in her throat.

A branding tool. Something that could burn into leather…or flesh.

"Robert?" Abby shook her head. There had to be a mistake. There had to be.

He reached past her, but she didn't move, unable to do anything but try to make sense of what was happening.

She lifted her gaze to his, ice sliding through her veins as she pointed to the object. "That's yours?"

He smiled, the practiced, casual smile she'd always thought telling of his good soul. The smile she now saw only as the outer manifestation of his inner evil.

Robert shrugged, his eyebrows lifting ever so slightly as if mocking her. "You want this to end? Here I am."

Disbelief flooded her system, her senses, numbing her to the shock of what she'd found, of what Robert said.

"You?"

"That's the thing about you, Abby." He stepped close, reaching into the drawer. "Even now, faced with the reality of what I am, you still don't see me at all, do you?"

What the hell was he talking about?

A madman. Jack's words bounced through her brain. *You can't force rationality on a madman.*

But she had to. Somehow. If she had any hope of surviving.

She'd thought herself so smart, coming to the office like this, wanting to lure the Christmas Confessor into the open, never guessing her own partner, her lifelong friend was harm personified—pure evil hidden behind a designer shirt and a smiling face.

The pieces of the puzzle came together, moving into focus inside her mind's eye.

The year Robert had spent out west after his father's death. His access to the blog. To the post office box.

To Abby.

To Gina.

To Natalie.

To everyone who had trusted him.

Bile clawed at the back of Abby's throat but she bit it back.

She longed to scream, to fight, to pummel him with her fists, and yet she did nothing. Nothing but process the reality of what her friend had done. The reality of the killer Robert was.

The reality of her fate. Then she thought again of the young police officer, knowing there had been no trip to the doughnut shop.

"What did you do to Officer Jones?"

Robert laughed then, a brief burst of emotionless air. "Let's just say you don't need to worry about him, shall we?

"I'm not entirely evil, Abby. Once I strangle *you,* the good news is, you won't feel a thing." He moved behind her and Abby closed her eyes, her mind frantic to seize upon a way out.

He squeezed her shoulders and Abby shuddered, the move once so familiar and comforting, now nothing but bone-chilling.

"We're going to take a little walk. I want to make sure no one interrupts my Christmas message. My final confession." He gave her shoulders another squeeze. "You, of course."

"I'll get you help, Robert. Don't do this. Please." She barely managed the words before he hit her, knocking her from her knees and onto the carpeted floor.

"You should have thought about being attentive when your life didn't depend on your actions." He blew out a fake sigh. "*That* would have been more convincing."

Stars swam in her vision and she reached for a stapler that had fallen, hoping to use it as a weapon. She had to stall Robert, had to keep him from killing her before Jack and the others had a chance to race across town.

And Abby had to believe that's what Jack was doing right now, she had to believe that the picture from Boone Shaw's belongings would be of Robert, and that Jack would realize the Christmas Confessor had been in their midst all along.

She had to believe Jack would reach her in time, had to believe he'd save her. She had to believe he loved her and would fight for her.

She had to.

She'd live to see Jack again, to feel his arms around her, holding her, keeping her safe. She'd see Jack again—or else she'd die trying.

Urgency filled her, renewing her strength. She reached for the stapler and swung.

Robert's foot connected with her wrist, sending the stapler flying from her grip and crashing to the floor.

Abby scrambled to her knees, fighting to gain her footing, to get to her feet, to move away from him. *Away from the monster she'd known all her life.*

She could think of nothing else.

Robert's foot connected with her back, pinning her to the floor and crushing her face to the carpet.

But then a noise sounded in the distance. Sirens. Blessed sirens.

He yanked her to her feet and shoved her toward the building's back exit.

His fingers cut into Abby's upper arm, his hold so tight no amount of squirming or fighting loosened his grip.

And as he shoved her through the back exit, snow swirled down from the December sky, spiraling onto the sidewalk illuminated by holiday lighting and lampposts.

Something glistened in Robert's hand and Abby realized what he'd reached for in the moment they'd moved away from his desk.

The branding tool.

And if she'd had any lingering hope before, reality crashed through her system now.

Robert Walker intended to make her his next victim.

His *Christmas message*.

Then he turned the corner, leading her down a street so familiar she could walk this route with her eyes shut. He was taking her to the one place no one expected her to be, the last place they'd look.

He was taking her home, to her home.

And Abby realized her only hope of survival now was a Christmas miracle…named Jack.

Chapter Seventeen

Something shimmered from beneath Robert Walker's desk.

Abby's cherry-red phone.

They were too late.

Jack's world spun momentarily. She wouldn't have gone anywhere with Robert voluntarily once she put the pieces together, as he had to believe she'd done.

Had Walker knocked the phone out of her hand? Or had she been trying to let Jack know there'd been a struggle.

Walker had her. But where?

"Every car in this city is looking for them, Jack." Hayes's voice sounded from just behind him. "I've got responders less than a minute from Walker's home address."

Less than a minute. If only.

Cold, raw fear sat in the pit of Jack's stomach. "We could already be too late."

"The bus is here, sir," a uniformed officer spoke from beside Hayes, his voice subdued.

They'd found Officer Jones upon their arrival, unconscious, but alive. Based on his recent killing spree, Robert Walker had showed mercy. Either that, or he hadn't had time to finish the job.

Tim Hayes's phone rang at the same moment Jack's

focus landed on a familiar object—the photo of Abby, Vicki and Gina. The photo that had gone missing from her apartment. Same frame, same faces.

"No one home at Walker's," Hayes said, stepping into Jack's line of vision, his expression frantic. "Ideas."

Jack nodded, having to appreciate the beauty of what Walker had done, of where he had taken Abby.

The man was smart, but Jack was smarter.

"I'll get the cars," Hayes said, stepping away.

Jack reached for him, grasping his elbow as he steered the man toward the door, breaking into a run.

"We won't need cars."

Right now, all they needed was time.

BILE CLAWED AT the back of her throat as Robert shoved her through her own front door. The one time she needed Dwayne Franklin's over-attentiveness, the man was long gone, behind bars and awaiting arraignment.

Robert shoved her against the wall, then bound her wrists and ankles with plastic ties. She fought against him, clawing, scratching, trying desperately to escape his hold, to avoid the ties, but he was stronger, faster, and before she knew it, she found herself fully bound and shoved to her knees, facing the wall.

"Nice Christmas lights, by the way."

Robert's voice set her teeth on edge, sent fear sluicing through her veins.

"You always did like the holidays, didn't you?" he continued. "I guarantee this year's will be your most memorable. Not that you'll remember it." He laughed, the sound cold and emotionless. "The public will remember though. Even more importantly, they'll remember me."

Abby twisted to face him, sitting down with her back

to the wall. She studied the face she'd thought she knew so well. "I trusted you."

"That was your first mistake." He pursed his lips.

"And my second?"

"Ignoring me."

"I never ignored you, Robert. You were my friend."

His laugh intensified, growing deeper, fuller, yet even colder. "You were never my friend. A friend doesn't call another friend a crank. A friend doesn't call another friend's life work and best photos self-serving attempts at sensationalism." Robert dropped to his knees, speaking so harshly he spit.

The image of Gina's lifeless body splayed across the bed filled Abby's mind. "Why Gina?"

He nodded, grinning. "Why not?"

Dread reached deep inside Abby and pulled tight. He kept talking without prompting, leaning close, so close the warmth of his breath brushed Abby's face, churning her insides.

"I killed Vicki."

Vicki.

Abby shook her head. "She killed herself. I saw her."

"How many women hang themselves, Abby? Grow up."

"Why?"

The word squeaked from Abby's throat, and a shudder ripped through her at the insanity of it all. The murders. The friendships. The lies.

Robert shrugged. "Oldest reason in the book. She figured me out."

Abby frowned, unable to speak or find her voice.

"You're scared." Robert nodded and licked his lips. "I like that. You deserve to be scared, Abby. You deserve to be very scared."

"What did she figure out?"

Abby wasn't sure how she formed the words, she just did. She had to if she wanted to survive. The longer she kept Robert talking, the greater the chance she'd get out of this alive. Somehow.

"She found my photos."

His photos. She'd forgotten somewhere along the way that Robert had once loved photography. Back in school they'd spend hours—she, Vicki and Gina—mugging for Robert after school, posing like movie stars for black-and-white shots that never went much further than the high school yearbook.

"I thought you gave that up when you went to college."

He shook his head, anger shimmering in his pale eyes. "Just another example of how little you pay attention."

He straightened, pacing a tight pattern in front of her. "I know about the phone call, by the way."

"The phone call?" Confusion whirled through Abby's brain.

"To you." He came to a stop, staring down into Abby's eyes, no doubt enjoying the position of power. "From Vicki."

Abby's mouth went so dry it might as well have been stuffed with cotton. No one knew about the call. She'd told no one.

"I was there, inside her house, waiting to kill her when she called you."

Abby said nothing.

"I'd just spoken to you, so I knew you were home," Robert continued. "I knew you'd ignored her, Abby." He leaned close again. "That wasn't very nice."

She shook her head. "I know."

"You weren't the only one, you know."

Abby fell silent again, not understanding what he was trying to say.

"She called Gina, too." He made a clucking sound with

his tongue. "Gina ignored her, too. So you see, you both failed your friend."

"But you killed her."

"But the guilt ate you alive. Not me." He laughed again, the sound chilling Abby to her core. "And I let it. Why not?" He shrugged. "You needed me after that, and you listened to me."

"You were my friend, Robert." And he had been. Or at least, so she'd thought. Abby's heart broke a bit more at the very ideas he'd never known her *friend* at all.

"But then the Web site took off and you forgot about me again." Robert's eyes narrowed, his features tensed. "You refuse to take me seriously, even after all this time."

"So you sent the postcard of Melinda."

"And you blew it off."

"You were the one who said it was a crank." Her voice climbed defensively and she hated herself for showing weakness.

Robert's smile widened. "I was playing to your stubbornness. I knew you'd take it and run."

"But I didn't." Realization dawned, sobering and heavy. She was to blame for setting everything into motion. She hadn't given Robert's confession enough print space.

"No." He shook his head. "You gave me one small blog and then you set me aside."

"Then Jack showed up."

Robert drew in a deep breath. "Detective Grant. Emma's picture was always one of my favorites."

"So you sent the second card."

"Went home at lunchtime to paste it together then tucked it inside your pocket."

"How did you know the mail was in my coat?"

He leaned so close his breath brushed her face and she cringed. "I, unlike other people I know, pay attention."

Why hadn't Abby paid more attention? Why hadn't she suspected Robert's involvement?

Because he was her friend.

Her heart gave a sharp twist. What a fool she'd been.

"What about Beverly Bricken?"

Robert shook his head and whistled. "I never expected that one."

"You didn't kill her?"

"Oh, I killed her. She was my one slip during all of those years, but her rejection of me was so harsh, she got what she deserved."

"But you didn't send the card?"

"That was Devine."

Abby blinked. "Did you know him?"

Another shake of the head. Another denial. "I knew of him. I was impressed, actually, that he took me seriously enough to copy the card."

"And that worked for you?"

Another nod. "Beautifully. Not so well, however, for Sam Devine."

Abby's brain whirled, racing against time to figure out a way to stop Robert from what he was about to do. She had to keep him talking, no matter how painful his admissions were to hear.

"Did you kill Boone Shaw?"

Abby's wrists and ankles throbbed from being bound so tightly. Sooner or later, her strength and determination weren't going to be enough to hold Robert off any longer.

"Let's just say I eased his suffering." Robert pulled a length of cord from his pocket, the same type of cord he'd left wrapped around Gina's neck. "Anything you want to confess before you die?"

Abby froze, saying nothing.

"Last chance?" He stepped close and unwrapped the

cord, anchoring either end around his hands and pulling the length taut.

"I'm sorry I ever thought you were my friend."

"That, Abby Conroy, makes two of us."

Robert made his move, shoving Abby off balance, then wrapping the cord around her throat.

Abby choked against the pressure, against the pain.

"I always knew what you needed, Abby. Remember that."

Then something shifted in his expression and he eased off on the pressure. He leaned close, his breath brushing Abby's face as he spoke.

"I wonder what it would be like to hear you beg for mercy as I take your body? Your life?"

He lowered one hand to her neck, trailing his fingers down the length of her skin to her throat, dipping his fingertips beneath the edge of her shirt, gently at first, then brusquely, cupping her breast and squeezing hard.

Abby's insides turned liquid and she squirmed beneath him, unable to break his hold.

Robert lowered his mouth to the hollow at her throat, pressing his lips to her flesh, the move anything but sensual, igniting raw fear inside her at the thought of the horrors he was about to inflict.

"Don't do this." She forced the words through her terror. "Please."

"You're not in charge anymore, Abby." He pushed back onto his heels, lowering the cord to the floor, reaching for the waistband of her jeans. "I am. And I'm about to make sure you remember that. Forever."

JACK SNEAKED AROUND the side of Abby's house, following the sidewalk. Light shone from the open door to her living room and voices filtered into the air outside.

Abby's voice. Frightened, but alive.

Relief rushed Jack's senses, but he concentrated on maintaining focus, on not letting his heart screw up his head.

The rest of the team had positioned themselves near the windows, and backup maneuvered up the same path, a few feet off of Jack's heels.

Jack raised his weapon as he peered around the corner of the steps. Walker squatted over Abby, undoing the waistband of her jeans.

Abby's feet and hands were bound—and the urge to kill Walker swelled in Jack's chest.

He could aim now, pull the trigger, and the man would pay the ultimate price for the lives he'd taken, the families he'd destroyed.

Abby struggled beneath Walker's touch, frantically trying to break free of the madman's hold.

Jack moved with lightning speed, barreling into Walker and slamming the man to the hardwood floor.

Jack pressed the barrel of his gun to the space between Walker's eyes and snarled, fighting the urge to pull the trigger.

"What are you going to do Jack, shoot me?"

Jack pressed the gun so firmly into Walker's skin his flesh turned white from the pressure of the gun's barrel.

He thought about pulling the trigger, thought about ending the life that didn't deserve to live, but he didn't.

He wasn't God, and he wasn't judge and jury.

He was a brother who had lost a sister, a detective who wanted justice, and a man who wanted the woman he loved to live to see the years of life ahead of her.

"It's over, Walker." The voice that spoke was Hayes's.

Walker, Jack and Abby were fully surrounded.

And the Christmas Confessor was finished.

Once and for all.

Epilogue

Abby had thought about shutting down Don't Say a Word. After all, she was alone now. She'd learned her failure to answer Vicki's call had in no way brought about her death—a murder Robert had committed in order to keep his dark secrets just that…secret.

Ironic for someone who had become Abby's partner in the confession site, yet that had been a lie, as well, nothing more than a way for Robert to gain Abby's attention. Though in his mind, it had been Abby who had failed him.

Abby opened her word processing program and stared at the blank screen then at the calendar.

Valentine's Day.

A typical mid-February snowstorm swirled outside her apartment window. She'd been unable to go back to the office. The specter of Natalie and Gina and Robert lurked around every corner.

Yet Abby hadn't been able to shut down the site. She hadn't been able to take away the outlet for those who needed it. She could only pray she'd never receive another postcard like the one that had set her nightmare into motion.

I didn't mean to kill her.

Abby's nightmare had been Jack's salvation, she supposed. He'd gone back to Arizona after Robert's arrest, after the evidence in Robert's apartment had all but sealed the fact he'd been the killer all along—the man Sam Devine had dubbed the Christmas Confessor.

Amidst the evidence found in Robert's home had been a diagram of a location in a remote section of New Mexico desert where he'd buried a trunk. In that trunk, the local police had found Melinda Simmons's remains. Her father had been given closure…at long last.

Abby knew that piece of the puzzle had haunted Jack, just as she knew the final resolution had provided him with satisfaction for a job well done.

Yet, he'd shut down that day. At the moment she'd expected his walls to crumble, they'd risen stronger than ever.

And then he'd walked out of her life.

Sam Devine's body had been shipped home for burial in a family plot in upstate New York. The media barely gave the reporter's murder notice. Even in death, Devine hadn't been able to grab the headlines he so craved.

The crime lab had concluded Devine had sent the third postcard himself, never realizing he'd feed into Robert Walker's master plan and motivate the man to kill again. Devine had also never figured he'd become one of Walker's final victims.

Boone Shaw's body had been located in a vacant lot in Elkton, Maryland. His widow had flown east to accompany her husband's body home.

While Shaw hadn't been able to expose the true killer's identity before his death, his actions had set into motion the chain of events that brought about Robert's downfall.

Robert had killed because he'd felt ignored. Ironically, his crimes had made him famous. Abby found herself haunted by the realization notoriety was what the man she'd once called friend had wanted all along, no matter the costs in human lives.

There had been one point during the days immediately following her brush with Robert Walker and death that Abby had thought Jack might stay in Delaware, or that he might ask her to go back to Arizona with him.

He'd done neither, leaving without so much as a glance back over his shoulder.

He'd closed the case and put his sister's death behind him just as easily as he'd put Abby behind him.

They'd spoken a few times since that day. About the case. About the victims. About closure. Yet, they'd never spoken about the intimacy they'd shared or about the possibility of a future together, much as Abby had hoped they might. She still held on to the hope Jack might show up on her doorstep one day, yet as the weeks passed, she realized that particular dream was fading fast.

For Abby, Jack Grant had unlocked far more than a case. He'd unlocked her heart.

What a fool she'd been.

The familiar ache squeezed at her chest, but Abby did her best to ignore it, focusing instead on the blank screen and the blog she needed to post.

She'd chosen a single postcard to feature this week. A grainy black-and-white photo of two small children holding hands, the message simple. Lost love. Missed opportunity. A lifetime of regret suffered in silence, but now shared for the world to see.

Abby supposed she could have confessed her feelings for Jack. She could have taken countless actions to let him know how she felt, and yet she'd done nothing.

She stared at the image on the postcard and thought of how she'd felt inside the safety of Jack's arms, how she'd felt to lay bare her soul to the man, how she'd felt to trust him fully.

She'd thought she'd come home…to Jack.

How wrong she'd been.

Here she sat, ready to share the confession of a stranger with the world, when it was her own secret that needed to be confessed.

She loved Jack. So what was she going to do about it?

A knock sounded at the door to her apartment and she jumped, startled by the sharp noise.

A young couple had moved into Dwayne's apartment. Perhaps they needed to borrow something, or perhaps they had a question about the neighborhood.

Abby drew in a deep breath then pushed away from her desk, away from her computer screen. She was only a few feet from the door when she saw the edge of the postcard slide across the sill.

The room spun and she reached for a chair to steady herself. She dropped to a squatting position, reaching for the card even as she questioned whether or not she should touch it.

What if Robert hadn't been the Confessor after all? What if he hadn't been operating alone? What if the nightmare was about to begin again?

"Cool it, Conroy," she told herself.

Robert would remain behind bars until the day he died.

Abby's fingertips brushed the edge of the card and she pulled it from beneath the door, her pulse quickening when she saw the photograph—a single red rose in a bud vase.

Slowly she turned the card in her hand, recognizing the handwriting instantly.

Can you ever forgive me?

A sob caught in her throat and she pushed to her feet, pulling the door open as quickly as she could.

Jack sat on the top step, his body angled so that he could see her, the shoulders of his leather jacket dusted with snow. A crooked smile pulled at one corner of his mouth.

"I thought you didn't believe in confessions?" she asked, her heart pounding against her ribs.

He pushed to his feet, brushed the snow off of his shoulders and shrugged. "I also said I didn't like snow."

"So you're saying you lied?" she teased.

His grin widened. "I'm saying I changed."

Abby swallowed, unable to believe Jack was real.

He took Abby's hands, his gaze locking on hers. "I was wrong to leave. I'm sorry."

Abby said nothing, holding her breath, not wanting to break the moment's spell.

"I thought you wanted me to fix things, to save you—"

"You did save me, Jack," she interrupted, unable to keep quiet any longer.

But Jack shook his head, his features softening. "You're wrong. You saved me." He squeezed her hands. "I don't want to live without you, Abby. I can't promise that I'll always be able to keep you safe or be the man you deserve, but I'd like to try. If you'll have me."

Abby blinked against the tears welling in her vision, not wanting to spoil the moment by dissolving into a sobbing mess.

"So?" Jack asked. "Do you have an answer for me? Can you forgive me?"

Abby nodded, relief and love rushing through her.

Jack pulled her into his arms and backed her into the apartment.

"Thank goodness," he said, his rich laughter heating Abby from head to toe. "I thought I might freeze out there."

"I think you secretly like the snow," Abby teased.

Jack kissed her slow and deep, then pulled back just enough to whisper, his lips brushing against hers as he spoke. "I hate the snow, but you, Abby Conroy? You, I love."

"I love you, too, Jack."

He kissed her again and this time, Abby broke their contact.

"Are you sure you don't want to go back outside? We could make a snowman."

He slid his hands down her arms, kicked the door shut, then steered Abby toward the bedroom. "Now you're just pushing your luck."

"I see." Abby's happy laughter mixed with Jack's as she studied his every feature, thinking she never wanted to be apart from the man again. "Maybe I should just welcome you home then."

And as they crossed the threshold into her bedroom and Jack hoisted her up onto the bed, he reached for the zipper on her sweatshirt drawing it slowly downward as he spoke, this time his voice husky and full of heat.

"Now that—" he pressed a kiss into the hollow of her throat then moved his mouth lower and lower still "—I could get used to."

* * * * *

Here is a sneak preview of
A STONE CREEK CHRISTMAS,
the latest in Linda Lael Miller's acclaimed
McKETTRICK *series.*

A lonely horse brought vet Olivia O'Ballivan to
Tanner Quinn's farm, but it's the rancher's love that
might cause her to stay.

A STONE CREEK CHRISTMAS
Available December 2008
from Silhouette Special Edition

Tanner heard the rig roll in around sunset. Smiling, he wandered to the window. Watched as Olivia O'Ballivan climbed out of her Suburban, flung one defiant glance toward the house and started for the barn, the golden retriever trotting along behind her.

Taking his coat and hat down from the peg next to the back door, he put them on and went outside. He was used to being alone, even liked it, but keeping company with Doc O'Ballivan, bristly though she sometimes was, would provide a welcome diversion.

He gave her time to reach the horse Butterpie's stall, then walked into the barn.

The golden retriever came to greet him, all wagging tail and melting brown eyes, and he bent to stroke her soft, sturdy back. "Hey, there, dog," he said.

Sure enough, Olivia was in the stall, brushing Butterpie down and talking to her in a soft, soothing voice that touched something private inside Tanner and made him want to turn on one heel and beat it back to the house.

He'd be damned if he'd do it, though.

This was *his* ranch, *his* barn. Well-intentioned as she was, *Olivia* was the trespasser here, not him.

"She's still very upset," Olivia told him, without turning to look at him or slowing down with the brush.

Shiloh, always an easy horse to get along with, stood contentedly in his own stall, munching away on the feed Tanner had given him earlier. Butterpie, he noted, hadn't touched her supper as far as he could tell.

"Do you know anything at all about horses, Mr. Quinn?" Olivia asked.

He leaned against the stall door, the way he had the day before, and grinned. He'd practically been raised on horseback; he and Tessa had grown up on their grandmother's farm in the Texas hill country, after their folks divorced and went their separate ways, both of them too busy to bother with a couple of kids. "A few things," he said. "And I mean to call you Olivia, so you might as well return the favor and address me by my first name."

He watched as she took that in, dealt with it, decided on an approach. He'd have to wait and see what that turned out to be, but he didn't mind. It was a pleasure just watching Olivia O'Ballivan grooming a horse.

"All right, *Tanner*," she said. "This barn is a disgrace. When are you going to have the roof fixed? If it snows again, the hay will get wet and probably mold…"

He chuckled, shifted a little. He'd have a crew out there the following Monday morning to replace the roof and shore up the walls—he'd made the arrangements over a week before—but he felt no particular compunction to explain that. He was enjoying her ire too much; it made her color rise and her hair fly when she turned her head, and the faster breathing made her perfect breasts go up and down in an enticing rhythm. "What makes you so sure I'm a greenhorn?" he asked mildly, still leaning on the gate.

At last she looked straight at him, but she didn't move

from Butterpie's side. "Your hat, your boots—that fancy red truck you drive. I'll bet it's customized."

Tanner grinned. Adjusted his hat. "Are you telling me real cowboys don't drive red trucks?"

"There are lots of trucks around here," she said. "Some of them are red, and some of them are new. And *all* of them are splattered with mud or manure or both."

"Maybe I ought to put in a car wash, then," he teased. "Sounds like there's a market for one. Might be a good investment."

She softened, though not significantly, and spared him a cautious half smile, full of questions she probably wouldn't ask. "There's a good car wash in Indian Rock," she informed him. "People go there. It's only forty miles."

"Oh," he said with just a hint of mockery. "*Only* forty miles. Well, then. Guess I'd better dirty up my truck if I want to be taken seriously in these here parts. Scuff up my boots a bit, too, and maybe stomp on my hat a couple of times."

Her cheeks went a fetching shade of pink. "You are twisting what I said," she told him, brushing Butterpie again, her touch gentle but sure. "I meant…"

Tanner envied that little horse. Wished he had a furry hide, so he'd need brushing, too.

"You *meant* that I'm not a real cowboy," he said. "And you could be right. I've spent a lot of time on construction sites over the last few years, or in meetings where a hat and boots wouldn't be appropriate. Instead of digging out my old gear, once I decided to take this job, I just bought new."

"I bet you don't even *have* any old gear," she challenged, but she was smiling, albeit cautiously, as though she might withdraw into a disapproving frown at any second.

He took off his hat, extended it to her. "Here," he teased. "Rub that around in the muck until it suits you."

She laughed, and the sound—well, it caused a powerful and wholly unexpected shift inside him. Scared the hell out of him and, paradoxically, made him yearn to hear it again.

* * * * *

Discover how this rugged rancher's wanderlust
is tamed in time for a merry Christmas, in
A STONE CREEK CHRISTMAS.
In stores December 2008.

SPECIAL EDITION™

FROM *NEW YORK TIMES* BESTSELLING AUTHOR

LINDA LAEL MILLER

A STONE CREEK CHRISTMAS

Veterinarian Olivia O'Ballivan finds the animals
in Stone Creek playing Cupid between her and
Tanner Quinn. Even Tanner's daughter, Sophie,
is eager to play matchmaker. With everyone
conspiring against them and the holiday season
fast approaching, Tanner and Olivia may just get
everything they want for Christmas after all!

*Available December 2008
wherever books are sold.*

Visit Silhouette Books at www.eHarlequin.com LLMNYTBPA

Silhouette
Desire

MERLINE LOVELACE

THE DUKE'S NEW YEAR'S RESOLUTION

Sabrina Russo is touring southern Italy when an accident places her in the arms of sexy Dr. Marco Calvetti. The Italian duke and doctor reluctantly invites her to his villa to heal…and soon after, he is vowing to do whatever he needs to keep her in Italy *and* in his bed….

Available December wherever books are sold.

Always Powerful, Passionate and Provocative.

Visit Silhouette Books at www.eHarlequin.com   SD76913

Harlequin® Historical
Historical Romantic Adventure!

THE MISTLETOE WAGER

Christine Merrill

Harry Pennyngton, Earl of Anneslea,
is surprised when his estranged wife,
Helena, arrives home for Christmas.
Especially when she's intent on
divorce! A festive house party
is in full swing when the guests
are snowed in, and Harry and
Helena find they are together
under the mistletoe....

*Available December 2008
wherever books are sold.*

HARLEQUIN® Romance®

Marry-Me Christmas

by *USA TODAY* bestselling author

SHIRLEY JUMP

A Bride FOR ALL *Seasons*

Ruthless and successful journalist Flynn never mixes
business with pleasure. But when he's sent to write a
scathing review of Samantha's bakery, her beauty and
innocence catches him off guard. Has this small-town
girl unlocked the city slicker's heart?

Available December 2008.

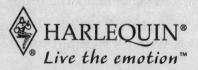

HARLEQUIN®
Live the emotion™

www.eHarlequin.com   HRI 7557

EXTRA

THE ITALIAN'S BRIDE

Commanded—to be his wife!

Used to the finest food, clothes and women, these immensely powerful, incredibly good-looking and undeniably charismatic men have only one last need: a wife!

They've chosen their bride-to-be and they'll have her—willing or not!

Enjoy all our fantastic stories in December:

THE ITALIAN BILLIONAIRE'S SECRET LOVE-CHILD
by CATHY WILLIAMS (Book #33)

SICILIAN MILLIONAIRE, BOUGHT BRIDE
by CATHERINE SPENCER (Book #34)

BEDDED AND WEDDED FOR REVENGE
by MELANIE MILBURNE (Book #35)

THE ITALIAN'S UNWILLING WIFE
by KATHRYN ROSS (Book #36)

www.eHarlequin.com

HPE1208

REQUEST YOUR FREE BOOKS!

**2 FREE NOVELS
PLUS 2
FREE GIFTS!**

HARLEQUIN®

INTRIGUE®

Breathtaking Romantic Suspense

YES! Please send me 2 FREE Harlequin Intrigue® novels and my 2 FREE gifts (gifts are worth about $10). After receiving them, if I don't wish to receive any more books, I can return the shipping statement marked "cancel." If I don't cancel, I will receive 6 brand-new novels every month and be billed just $4.24 per book in the U.S. or $4.99 per book in Canada, plus 25¢ shipping and handling per book and applicable taxes, if any*. That's a savings of close to 15% off the cover price! I understand that accepting the 2 free books and gifts places me under no obligation to buy anything. I can always return a shipment and cancel at any time. Even if I never buy another book from Harlequin, the two free books and gifts are mine to keep forever.

182 HDN EEZ7   382 HDN EEZK

Name _____ (PLEASE PRINT)

Address _____ Apt. #

City _____ State/Prov. _____ Zip/Postal Code

Signature (if under 18, a parent or guardian must sign)

Mail to the **Harlequin Reader Service:**
IN U.S.A.: P.O. Box 1867, Buffalo, NY 14240-1867
IN CANADA: P.O. Box 609, Fort Erie, Ontario L2A 5X3

Not valid to current subscribers of Harlequin Intrigue books.

**Want to try two free books from another line?
Call 1-800-873-8635 or visit www.morefreebooks.com.**

* Terms and prices subject to change without notice. N.Y. residents add applicable sales tax. Canadian residents will be charged applicable provincial taxes and GST. Offer not valid in Quebec. This offer is limited to one order per household. All orders subject to approval. Credit or debit balances in a customer's account(s) may be offset by any other outstanding balance owed by or to the customer. Please allow 4 to 6 weeks for delivery. Offer available while quantities last.

Your Privacy: Harlequin is committed to protecting your privacy. Our Privacy Policy is available online at www.eHarlequin.com or upon request from the Reader Service. From time to time we make our lists of customers available to reputable third parties who may have a product or service of interest to you. If you would prefer we not share your name and address, please check here. ☐

HI08R

Inside ROMANCE

Stay up-to-date on all your romance reading news!

The Inside Romance newsletter is a FREE quarterly newsletter highlighting our upcoming series releases and promotions!

Click on the <u>Inside Romance</u> link on the front page of **www.eHarlequin.com** or e-mail us at insideromance@harlequin.ca to sign up to receive your FREE newsletter today!

You can also subscribe by writing us at: HARLEQUIN BOOKS
Attention: Customer Service Department
P.O. Box 9057, Buffalo, NY 14269-9057

Please allow 4-6 weeks for delivery of the first issue by mail.

IRN-IBPA208

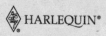

HARLEQUIN®
INTRIGUE®
COMING NEXT MONTH

#1101 CHRISTMAS DELIVERY by Patricia Rosemoor
A Holiday Mystery at Jenkins Cove
Lexie Thornton gave up on romance after the love of her life was killed at an early age. But when Simon Shea mysteriously returned, Lexie's world turned upside down. Could Simon help Lexie unlock the secrets surrounding their pasts?

#1102 CHRISTMAS CRIME IN COLORADO by Cassie Miles
When Brooke Johnson found herself the target of a serial killer, it was up to police detective Michael Shaw to protect her. But then their professional relationship turned personal, and Michael knew survival depended on Brooke escaping the memories of her tragic past.

#1103 HIGH SCHOOL REUNION by Mallory Kane
Once Ultimate Agent Laurel Gillespie uncovered a ten-year-old clue that a former classmate's suicide may have been murder, her high school reunion turned deadly. With the help of former crush police chief Cade Dupree, Laurel was determined to solve the case, even if it meant losing Cade's affection—or her life.

#1104 THE MISSING MILLIONAIRE by Dani Sinclair
Harrison Trent's life was abruptly interrupted when beautiful Jamie Bellman claimed to be his bodyguard. To protect Harrison from the strange attacks, Jamie would risk everything—even losing her heart.

#1105 TALL, DARK AND LETHAL by Dana Marton
Thriller
With dangerous men hot on his trail, the last thing Cade Palmer needed was attractive Bailey Preston seeking his help to escape from attackers of her own. Could Cade tame the free-spirited Bailey as they fled both their enemies and the law?

#1106 A BODYGUARD FOR CHRISTMAS by Donna Young
The clues to Jordan Beck's hunt for his father's killers lay in the mind of beautiful bookseller Regina Menlow. With time running out, would Jordan and Regina be able to expose the terrorist who planned to wreak nuclear havoc on Christmas day?